MOONSTRUCK

Tony Harmsworth

Reader Club

Sign up for Tony's no-spam Reader Club newsletter for exclusive content, and special offers.

Details can be found at the end of MOONSTRUCK.

Copyright and Thanks to:

Wendy Harmsworth, Melanie Underwood

Also, thanks to these VIP Beta Reader Club Members: Mario Alman, Gabrielle Blaze, Robert W Brinkman, Annette Burgess, Anne Graham, David Green, Greg Hills, Dean Howard, James McCarthy, Connie Moon, Colin Pain, Joe Pedreiro, Mike Ramay, Nev Rawlins, Linda Reed, Toni Rizzo, Nigama Ranganatha, Patrick Stakem, who have contributed so much to my story.

ISBN: 9798600108486

Published by:
Harmsworth.net
Drumnadrochit
Inverness-shire
IV63 6XJ

1 An Almighty Rush

Note for non-British readers – Tony writes using UK English spelling, punctuation and grammar, plus some US English words where appropriate. Miles and kilometres will both be used in the story.

*It is **strongly** recommended that you read Moonscape before starting this sequel. Thank you.*

'If we don't stop arguing, we'll have lost the moon!' said Neil Weston, NASA's mission director for Project Moonstruck, the expedition to regain control of Moonbase from the alien entities.

The heads of NASA, Roscosmos, and CNSA, the Chinese space administration, looked around at Neil, who was ranked several levels below them.

'Dr Weston,' said Bob Michaels, severely. 'We must sort out the costs and responsibilities.'

Bob was head of NASA and also Neil's boss. He needed to speak less passionately to him. 'But every two days that we sit here arguing about who should pay for what, those things are replicating on the moon – doubling their number. By the end of this week, we should have the means to destroy them but we need to act quickly or there will be so many that we'll be overwhelmed.' I was sitting beside Neil and nodded in support.

In faltering English, Nicholas Melopov, a short rotund man in his mid-forties said, 'But, Dr Weston, there no evidence that the Lunar Regolith Parasites (LRPs) reproduce in absence of hosts. To our awareness, there be just five of them, perhaps six if Blake Smith survived.'

I said, ‘There is evidence! We know Dr MacIntosh extracted one from Roy Williams and then dropped it on the floor of one of the wards. We captured it and it lived in a sealed vacuum flask for several days before escaping and infecting me.’

‘Yes,’ said Lien Liu, a severe-looking, short, stocky Chinese woman in her sixties. ‘But the LRP didn’t reproduce on its own during that period.’

‘Correct,’ said Neil, ‘but we believe it wasn’t a full-strength parasite when it was removed from Mr Williams. We mustn’t take the chance that the LRPs could be reproducing outside the hosts. The mission timing is more important than the cost.’

I said, ‘We do know that each of the victims can produce a new LRP every two days and, if there are five of them, that means there are already dozens of LRPs and, if Blake Smith survived, perhaps a hundred plus. They could easily store the replicated LRPs somewhere.’

‘We aren’t just sitting here talking, you know,’ said Lien, looking at Neil and me. ‘We already have one ship ready for launch and a second should be available by the eleventh of April.’

‘We will also have two by that time,’ said the Russian.

Bob Michaels, a tall, gangly fifty-year-old, leaned back in his chair, ‘Okay. Neil has a point, but as Miss Liu says, we are all preparing for the mission. SpaceX has two new Dragonstar lunar landers already in Earth orbit. When the crews head for the moon, they will fly alongside us under remote control. That will make six landers in total which we can use to travel from the Lunar Orbiting Platform to the surface.'

Neil added, 'We've also suspended all unmanned flights to Copernicus and postponed mining crew flights indefinitely. We don't want to be supplying the aliens with useful materials.'

'How radiation projectors come along?' asked Nicholas.

'Final test this Friday,' I replied. 'Once we know they work, it won't take long to make a couple of dozen. The biggest problem, so I'm told by the lead scientist, was working out exactly what killed the LRP. The Van Allen belts contain such a toxic cocktail of particles and interactions that they had to use elimination to discover exactly what did the damage.'

'But they have?' asked Bob.

'Well, they checked the detectors on the Orion and narrowed down the radiations to the only ones which didn't penetrate regolith nor were commonly encountered on the moon's surface. That only left a couple of radiation types which could have been the fatal ones. The projectors will emit both.'

'And they're sure they are the right ones?'

'Yes, they're pretty sure,' I said. 'The test on Friday will tell us if the number of harmful particles the projectors emit is at a similar level to the maximum dose for them without damaging us too much. I don't understand the detail, I'm afraid.'

'What about effective range?' asked Nicholas.

'Not good,' I said. 'Only three or four metres, but they are also working on a multi-directional projector which will concentrate the same radiations, over a shorter timeframe. That will be effective over a much larger area, but still won't penetrate walls, et cetera. To penetrate solid structures, we'd have to add radiation which would be far too harmful to humans. The Van Allen belts are not good for us when we pass through them, even when shielded. We've had to be quite selective in choosing the radiations we use. The experts can provide more information than I.'

Wearily, Michaels leaned forward. 'Since we need the military folks and scientists to determine these factors,' he said, 'let's reconvene tomorrow morning. I know we have all been putting in long hours, but we need to be as focused and as fresh as we possibly can and Dr Weston and Dr Noble have a press conference to attend.'

∞∞∞∞∞∞∞∞∞∞∞

Neil and I headed straight to the Johnson Space Center where a news conference was going to take place that afternoon.

The *Chicago Tribune* had somehow got hold of the story and released it the previous day. It had caused an explosion of interest which couldn't be ignored or denied. NASA decided that Neil should handle the flak but would take me along to talk about the effect of the parasites on humans. This promised to be a lively affair. The agency had wanted to maintain secrecy, but when the Chinese returned to Earth from their Ben Lei habitat, it was realised that the moon had been abandoned, but for six individuals who made no contact. It didn't take long for the media to find out about the LRPs. Their digging finally hit a raw nerve and one of the medics at the Wilmington Hospital, where I had been treated, blew the whistle.

By restricting the press conference to one mission director and one astronaut, it was hoped the real danger could be underplayed. Personally, I'd have preferred to see more honesty and less manipulation.

We walked onto the stage and sat behind a desk bristling with microphones. In front of us, a sea of journalists' faces; among them, television and still cameras, handheld and on tripods.

Neil said, 'I have a short, prepared statement which I will read to you now and you can also collect a copy from the pile here on the desk.' He tapped the pile, took a copy from the top and began to read, 'On the sixteenth of February, astronauts Mark Noble and Roy Williams were surveying Timocharis Delta crater. An entity, which we call the Lunar Regolith Parasite or LRP, was apparently hibernating in deep dust until it was disturbed during the survey. It became attached to the moon buggy wheel and was inadvertently taken back to Moonbase.

'Once in the garage dome, it attacked geologist Roy Williams, overpowering him in seconds. It so effectively restrained Williams' bodily functions that the rest of the crew, including the Moonbase doctor, believed him to be dead.

'In fact, the LRP had taken control of Williams' mind and body. Presumed dead, he was left in the cold store to await a post-mortem.

The LRP, using Williams' body, attempted to escape Moonbase. We don't think it understood the nature of the habitat. Leaving the base, perhaps to conceal itself outside, was never going to be effective, as it would be easy to track the buggy.

'Noble and Dr MacIntosh followed the buggy. Williams was found and returned to Moonbase and, although quarantined, he appeared to have recovered.'

I said, 'He seemed slightly odd to me, but only because I knew him so well.'

A journalist called out, 'What do you mean by odd?'

'Hold on now,' said Neil. 'Let me finish the prepared statement and then we'll take questions.'

He continued, 'The Moonbase doctor, while examining Williams, broke quarantine and was also infected, although no one realised it at the time. Williams' entity had divided. This showed that the LRP was able to reproduce and was probably intelligent or it wouldn't have worked so hard to conceal its infection of the doctor. It was learning about our thought processes and likely actions.

'Two days later, the doctor transferred one of his own divided LRPs into astronaut Jennifer Hudson, and the two of them contrived to have the second new LRP from Williams dropped in the old ward where Williams had been kept initially. The rest of the crew found it and isolated it, thinking it was the original LRP and that Williams was now free of infection. He was kept in quarantine, but the rest of the crew were still unaware of the doctor's and Hudson's infections.

'Later that day, when it was eventually discovered that three of the crew were infected, NASA called upon military advisers who advised Blake Smith, the Moonbase commander, how to proceed. The three infected astronauts were caught and imprisoned in the medical centre.

'However, during the capture process, MacIntosh and Hudson had deposited two more LRPs in the com dome. During the night they took possession of Crystal Mitumba and either Deputy Commander Mary Carter or Commander Smith. They freed the three from the medical centre and Williams infected the remaining crew member in the com dome, leaving only Linda and Mark Noble uninfected. At the time, they were in their quarters.'

Neil had avoided mentioning that we weren't married at that time. He'd told me that he didn't want the media to make a fuss over single astronauts cohabiting on the moon.

'The next morning,' Neil continued, 'the Nobles were attacked by Williams, but Mark managed to incapacitate him. They grabbed the container which had the specimen parasite within it and fled for the Dragonstar with Smith and Williams in pursuit.

'During the Dragonstar countdown, Commander Smith and Williams arrived and tried to board the lander. Mark broke Smith's faceplate as he reached the hatch, and they were able to blast off. We are assuming Smith died but cannot be certain.

'Linda and Mark made it to the LOP and…'

'What's an LOP?' shouted one of the press.

'LOP,' I said, 'stands for the Lunar Orbiting Platform, the space station which orbits the moon, the way-station for moon landings, also referred to as the Lunar Gateway or just Gateway.'

Neil continued, 'They then transferred to an Orion and headed back to Earth. The LRPs, normally two or three inches long, have the ability to squeeze through the tiniest gaps. The specimen in the vacuum flask managed to escape during the flight and infected Mark. This happened just too late for Linda to abort the landing and burn-up the Orion during re-entry. The capsule was already on automatic control.'

'Wait a minute,' shouted one of the journalists. 'This thing is so dangerous that you were going to destroy yourselves?'

'Let me finish the statement,' said Neil.

'During Earth approach, the Orion passed briefly through the Van Allen belts and the radiation within the inner belt killed the parasite. It had been weakened as the Orion passed through the outer belt.

'It would be fair to say that the world would have been in real peril if it hadn't been killed. We now know that LRPs cannot tolerate the decay of neutrons caused by certain cosmic ray interactions in the inner Van Allen belt and we have built a projector, a sort of cosmic ray gun, which we believe can be used to destroy them with the same radiation, without killing the host.

'Early in April a combined US, Russian and Chinese Mission will be sent to clear Moonbase of the parasites and also reclaim the Chinese Ben Lei habitat. That mission will be led by Commander Mark Noble. Now, questions?' We both looked up at the audience.

'How sure are you that Commander Noble is clear of infection?'

'One hundred per cent. Next,' said Neil.

'Are they really so dangerous, you'd have killed yourselves to stop them getting to Earth?'

'Absolutely,' I said. 'Linda had just relinquished control to the computers when she realised that I'd been infected. She tried to override the system but was unable to do so.'

'Why would they be a serious threat to the Earth?'

Neil replied, 'The LRPs' ability to divide and infect every two days might not seem too threatening at first glance, but think on this – two, four, eight, sixteen, thirty-two, sixty-four, one hundred and twenty-eight, and that is the first two weeks. We've calculated that everyone in the world could be infected within three months.'

Concerned murmuring arose from the press.

'What happens on infection?' asked one of them.

'Total control,' I replied. 'The first thing it does is paralyse your speech centres so that you cannot shout out. Movement is controlled within a second. The next thing I felt was that it was learning how to move my arms, hands and other limbs. There is nothing you can do to stop it. As I tried to speak or move, it showered me with pain, first like red-hot needles, then equivalent to being sprayed with acid and finally it was letting me experience the agony of having my limbs, eyes and tongue ripped from my body. It was truly agony and I lost consciousness, despite having quite a high pain threshold. I can honestly say that it was a dreadful experience and one which I would never want to repeat.'

There was now a more open chat in the roomful of journalists.

'How did they remove it?' someone asked eventually.

'Cut it out,' I said and tapped my head. 'I now have a titanium plate in my skull.'

'So, if you are able to kill the LRPs, how are you going to get them out of the infected people on the moon?'

'In the crew,' said Neil, 'will be two theatre nurses, an anaesthetist and a brain surgeon. Most of the equipment including a CT scanner is in Moonbase, although some other items will be taken on the flight. There's a small surgery at Moonbase which can be made sterile.'

'So, invasive surgery. Is that the only way?' asked the journalist from the *Washington Post*.

'No,' I said. 'Using the scanner to monitor the situation, as long as the LRP is dead and visible between the skull and brain, as was the case with mine, keyhole surgery can be used to enter the body under either ear and extract the creature through the same opening. That would rely on the dead LRP being clear of the brain tissue. They couldn't use the keyhole system on me owing to urgency. Mine seemed to extract itself from my brain while it was dying so was lying against the inside of my skull.'

'Why on Earth would it do that?' asked the same journalist.

'We think it was trying to escape my body, but, frankly, we really don't know,' I said.

'When does the expedition depart?'

Neil answered, 'We are hoping to arrive at the Gateway by the fifteenth of April. The fleet will be two Ming ships containing four astronauts each; two Uspekhs, each with three Russian astronauts; two unmanned Dragonstar landers, we already have four at the Gateway; and two Orions carrying five astronauts and one carrying four. Twenty-eight of us in total.'

'And Mark Noble is commanding the expedition?'

‘Yes,’ said Neil. ‘That has been agreed and the twenty-seven other astronauts will be arriving at the Johnson Space Center for training in about a week.’

‘What’s the plan?’ asked a lady from the *New York Post*.

‘Sorry,’ I said. ‘That’s the classified element.’

Questions went on for the best part of an hour. NASA, in its usual way, trying to be as open as possible.

2 Space Force

The astronauts were beginning to arrive. A buffet lunch was set out in one of the lower assembly rooms at the Johnson Space Center. My wife Linda and I were there early to ensure everything needed would be to hand. My function would be to knit the force together so that we could act as one when we arrived on the moon. Linda was responsible for Dragonstar training and would be working with the pilots who would take us from the Gateway to the surface. She, of course, was grounded owing to some irresponsible freefall lovemaking in lunar orbit during our frantic journey to escape the infected crew just over a month previously.

'Hi, you two,' said Neil as he entered the assembly room with some of the NASA astronauts and others I only recognised from images.

'Hi, Neil,' said Linda.

'Sorry you're going to miss out on this gig,' he replied. 'Let me introduce you, although you'll know most of the crew.'

Neil waved for the new arrivals to come over to us.

'I'm sure you'll all know Mark Noble who will be mission commander,' said Neil. 'Linda Fuller… sorry, Noble – they married last week – will be responsible for Dragonstar training. You will all continue to work with your own Orion training teams.' He began announcing the names of each of the team.

I knew Dave Morgan, Pete Hazel, Anna Stanbury and Penny Heston from my own training group. Linda would not be pleased to see that Penny was on the squad. When I'd had a one-night fling with her about a year ago, it caused Linda and me to break up until she forgave me at Moonbase in January.

I'd been introduced to Colonel Doug Baker and Captain Mike Robertson earlier. They were to be in command of the international military personnel under my supervision. Anna, a brilliant pilot, was to be my deputy. Bill Wright was to be my independent military adviser and confidant provided by NASA for that purpose.

'Nice to see you guys again. Which of you have experience?' I asked. I knew full well who had done what, but this gave each of them a chance to break the ice with the group, which had now been joined by the six Russians and four of the Chinese.

'ISS twice,' said Dave, a white Brit with sandy hair.

'Moonbase – one tour,' said Pete, an Indonesian mixed race with very gentle features.

'Me too,' said Anna, a white brunette. 'Orion and Dragonstar pilot.'

'Excellent, Anna,' said Linda. 'I could do with some help on Dragonstar training.'

'ISS, one tour,' said Penny, colouring slightly as she spoke. Like Linda, she was a stunning petite platinum blonde. Hence Linda's annoyance.

‘And the rest of you – some have familiar faces but give us all a breakdown of what you’ve been doing,’ I said.

‘I’m Bill Wright, ex-army, now training for Moonbase,’ said a tall, heavily-built, but not overweight black man of Afro-Caribbean origin. He looked very no-nonsense and efficient. Neil had chosen him to offer specialist military advice to me. We’d met once and had got on really well.

‘Krishna Mishra, neuro-surgeon. Never flown,’ said a slight, nervous Indian man in his thirties.

‘I’ve never had to cut open a skull,’ I said. ‘Don’t look so anxious.’

‘Worried about space-sickness,’ he admitted.

‘Well, you’ll be fine on the moon and we’ll look after you en route,’ said Anna.

Also, in the group were the anaesthetist and two theatre nurses, none of whom had been in space.

Three of the Chinese astronauts were military, one of whom was a trained pilot. A fourth, Chi, was a very experienced astronaut and both a Ming and Dragonstar pilot.

Four of the six Russians were military. The other two were experienced Uspekh and Dragonstar pilots. One had served a tour at Moonbase and the other at the Chinese habitat.

The remainder of the military were US Marines and British commandos.

‘I’m very pleased to have met you all,’ I said. ‘I’m sure that all of your names will eventually stick. Don’t hesitate to tell me if I make mistakes.’

‘Help yourselves to the buffet,’ said Neil. ‘Mark and I will then take you to the theatre and we’ll run through the strategy.’

The buffet soon looked as if it had been struck by a plague of locusts and the chatter changed from introductions to stories of lives lived and visits made to orbit or the moon.

∞∞∞∞∞∞∞∞∞∞∞

Four weeks intense training, including several vomit-comet flights, gave us a good idea who would or wouldn’t be comfortable in freefall. We lost only two, sadly an experienced Marine and a British commando, but there was no shortage of volunteers to replace them.

The last evening, Linda and I made a point of having a quiet dinner, leaving the other Orion astronauts to enjoy an evening’s leisure. The Russians and Chinese had returned home by private jet, and the mass launch was scheduled for the tenth of April. We would be at the Gateway by the fifteenth as long as we didn’t run into any serious delays.

‘Don’t like the way *she* looks at you,’ said Linda

‘Nothing is going to happen,’ I said, holding her hand. ‘I was foolish when we were just dating. We weren’t exclusive then. I love you.’

She still didn't look happy. 'I thought we *were* exclusive!'

I tried to reassure her. 'We're married. She never meant anything to me. You trust me, don't you?'

'It's not you I don't trust, it's *her*! I can't help but notice the way she looks at you and the way she stands when she's near you… *and* all the blushing when she talks to you.'

'I promise. You know you don't really need to worry. That was a long time ago and it was before we'd committed to each other. Let's not spoil tonight talking about her.'

The subject changed and we talked about more domestic matters and preparations for becoming a proper family. The apartment wasn't suitable for a young family and we'd need to upsize during the pregnancy. The mission could be five months, by the time we sorted out the mess at Moonbase. The infected crew had smashed the equipment in the com dome, and it would take time to repair. When I returned to Earth, Linda would be almost ready to give birth.

We didn't want to waste our last night together, and our romantic dinner ended exactly as might be expected.

∞∞∞∞∞∞∞∞∞∞∞

Three Orions sat at the Kennedy Space Center. Never before had there been three simultaneous launches. Well, in fact they wouldn't be quite at the same time. One of the Orions was mounted on a SpaceX Heavy. It would be leaving shortly. The other two Orions, mounted on the NASA SLS (Space Launch System) rockets would launch an hour and ninety minutes after the SpaceX. A huge crowd had been gathering over the last few days.

We'd heard that the two Mings were successfully in orbit already, as was one of the two Uspekhs. The other was due to launch any minute.

I was in the last Orion to fly, with Bill Wright, Doug Baker, Mike Robertson, Gillian Atwell and our flight commander, Anna Stanbury. Although these Orions had been re-equipped to hold up to six, the radiation projectors were quite bulky and a lot of supplies were flying with us, enough for up to thirty-six people for six months. It would be an uncomfortable squeeze until we reached the Gateway.

We sat in the departure area, watching the countdown for the SpaceX Heavy. There was a hold at one-minute. NASA would be tying in with the SpaceX administration to ensure there was a smooth rendezvous with the two Dragonstar vessels. SpaceX would then link the command systems so that the Orion and Dragonstars could set off for the moon in formation.

All of the other craft would leave Earth orbit independently. The mechanics of orbital manoeuvring made formation flying virtually impossible when in space without computers being linked. All space pilots had at some time experienced extreme amusement when watching fleets of space fighters holding formation in the

Star Wars and *Star Trek* films. It just wasn't possible in reality.

'Two, ignition, zero and lift-off of the SpaceX Heavy,' was announced and we watched the huge stack setting off over the Atlantic towards northern Africa, the crackle of the jets sounding like a million simultaneous Roman candles being fired. Spectacular to watch. The three boosters would return to Earth once their job was done.

We were next to go. The flight director entered the departure area and we all rose, already in our flight suits, and made our way to pad thirty-nine. The others were launching from pad six.

Orions were spacious compared with the old Soyuz and Apollo capsules, but not so much with so many on board. Anna and I sat in the guidance seats with the remaining crew behind us. Once the outer door was sealed, the countdown began, although we would still have nearly an hour to wait.

During the interval, I ran through the last week in my mind. The cosmic ray-guns were easy enough to use, but of course we'd had no way to be one hundred per cent certain they'd work. As with most NASA projects, one had to have trust in the scientists' expertise. Everyone understood the importance of care in the operation and that it was the responsibility of all of us to ensure the medical crew were protected.

Ten minutes. Anna and I were now busy with the last part of countdown, listening to mission control and checking and cross-checking the data on our screens.

One minute. There is a huge anticipation and tension which begins to build in the final sixty seconds, and at that point the countdown is too advanced to be stopped. The only thing we could do now, if something went wrong, would be to fire the emergency escape rockets. The SLS stack beneath us would then become a multi-million-pound firework with our section struggling to keep ahead of the exploding gasses.

Three, two, ignition, zero and lift-off.

We were kicked in the back by enormous forces as the rocket cleared the tower and began its climb to orbit.

Telemetry was good, angle of lift-off was perfect, acceleration nominal. After a minute, I heard Anna confirming the ship was throttling back as we passed through maximum dynamic pressure, then those four unforgettable words from mission control.

'Orion 1. Go with throttle up!'

'Go with throttle up,' Anna repeated, and we felt the g-forces rise again as maximum thrust was applied.

This was the point during launch at which the space shuttle Challenger had exploded and I'm sure all of us had a thought about the lost astronauts as we moved smoothly onwards towards orbit but probably gripping our armrests a little more tightly.

‘Confirm booster separation,’ said Anna and we all felt a little less heavy now that it was only the main stack firing. The boosters had been jettisoned and were falling back to land at Cape Canaveral.

Later, Anna warned, ‘Prepare for staging.’

All thrust ceased and we were thrown forward. Bill had loosened his harness and his helmet hit the panel in front of him. We were, for just a few seconds getting a taste of freefall, then the third stage cut in and we were slammed backwards into our seats.

The third stage fired for less than two minutes then cut out. We were in rendezvous orbit.

‘Orbit achieved,’ said mission control.

‘Orbit confirmed,’ said Anna.

‘Neil, do you copy?’ I said.

‘Copy you, Mark.’

‘Everyone in orbit okay?’

‘No problems. Orion 3 has linked computers with the two Dragonstars. We’re just checking all of the orbits and we’ll give each of you a specific go for trans-lunar injection,’ said Neil.

‘No change in order?’

‘No. You first then Orion 3, Uspekh 1, Ming 1, Uspekh 2, Orion 2 and Ming 2.’

‘Thanks, Neil,’ I said, cut the connection and joined the others in enjoying the view of our beautiful planet from orbit.

3 Character Refresher

[This is a reference list. Please skip to chapter 4 if not required.]

Atwell, Gillian –white Marine – communications specialist

Baker, Doug – Marine colonel – tall, red-haired Caucasian – the senior military commander of the Marines, forty, well built

Carter, Mary – infected during Moonscape. Brilliant astrophysicist who was deputy commander of Moonbase – a forty-year-old woman of Pakistani extraction

Deskov, Mikhail – white Russian Marine sergeant

Dyson, John – white British Cockney commando, short and well built

Flowers, Darren – Afro-Caribbean Marine

Gilby, General – senior US general

Hazel, Pete – Moonbase once – mixed race
Dragonstar pilot

Heston, Penny – ISS once. Dragonstar pilot – had an affair with Mark, long before Moonscape – platinum blonde

Huang, Chan – Ming and Dragonstar Pilot, thirty-four

Hudson, Jenny – infected during Moonscape – a diminutive, early-thirties, Korean – in a relationship with Crystal Mitumba

Indlikova, Zoya – white Russian Marine – very athletic

Jones, Vicky – white Marine

Kane, Jack – black operating theatre nurse, jovial nature

Krupin, Andrei – Uspekh and Dragonstar pilot

Li, Lucy – Chinese Marine/commando

Liu, Lien – head of CNSA

MacIntosh, John (Tosh) – infected during Moonscape – senior Moonbase doctor with a background as a surgeon and in general practice. Swarthy, white, about fifty, argumentative

Mackay, Danny – white Marine, hefty

Melopov, Nicholas – head of Roscosmos

Michaels, Dr Bob – head of NASA

Mitumba, Crystal – infected during Moonscape – slim, tall, jet-black woman of Ghanaian origin – geologist – in a relationship with Jenny Hudson

Mesolvic, Vlad – white Russian Marine, hefty with red hair

Mills, Diana – white operating theatre nurse

Mishra, Krishna – Indian descent – brain surgeon – small build – head of the four strong medical team

Mirislov, Alexei – anaesthetist

Morgan, Dave – experienced astronaut who had had two stints at the ISS – white with sandy hair

Noble, Linda nee Fuller – Caucasian, golden blonde hair – fashion model figure – escaped with Mark Noble at the end of Moonscape – now married to him – grounded as expecting a child

Noble, Mark – tall, mid-thirties, medium build with dark wavy hair – senior geologist and now Moonbase commander – escaped with Linda Fuller at the end of Moonscape – married to her. This novel series is his story.

Olsson, Ludvic – white Russian Uspekh and Dragonstar pilot, athletic

Robertson, Mike – white Marine captain, deputy to Doug Baker

Smith, Blake – infected during Moonscape – he had been Moonbase commander – white, bad tempered

Stott, Jimmy – white Marine good-looking, tall and fit.

Stanbury, Anna – short white brunette with huge blue eyes. Had been at Moonbase prior to the Moonscape novel and had also had a short period as commander – senior Orion and Dragonstar pilot

Volkov, Ivan – white Russian Marine

Wang, Chi – experienced astronaut and both Ming and Dragonstar pilot – senior Chinese astronaut

Weston, Neil mission director at NASA

Williams, Roy – the first infected astronaut during Moonscape – geologist – best friend and colleague of Mark Noble – white

Wright, Bill – crew Dragon pilot – heavily built, British commando, Afro-Caribbean black man designated military advisor to Mark

Zhao, Ai – Chinese Marine

Buggy one computer: Selena

Buggy two computer: Bedford

Buggy three computer: Cavor

4 Trans Lunar Flight

Do you ever look at the moon on a clear evening? It is marvellous to think about how it affects our tides and the lives of the myriad animals that live on Earth. However, as someone who has been there and walked on the lunar surface, what I find most amazing is that we are able to get there at all.

In the vastness of space, it is such a tiny object and so far away. It is moving around its orbit of Earth at over two thousand miles per hour and we have to fire our rockets to complete our journey to arrive where the moon will then be forty-eight hours later, by which time it will have travelled around one hundred thousand miles. If we misjudge our trajectory, we will miss the moon completely and be heading away into the solar system with no way to return.

When we arrive in lunar orbit, there will be a short burn to slow us down and then we have to rendezvous with the Gateway, a space station no larger than a detached house, which is travelling in an eccentric orbit at thousands of miles per hour.

I'm not a pilot, but I have unqualified admiration for those who are responsible for the calculations which lead to a successful lunar orbit. How the Apollo lunar module crews managed to rendezvous with their command modules, armed only with the equipment they had in the sixties, never ceases to amaze me.

Orbital mechanics is not as easy as most people would like to imagine. In the early sixties, spacecraft missed each other by hundreds of miles when trying to rendezvous. Eventually, Buzz Aldrin managed to work out how to rendezvous in orbit and he wrote the handbook which today makes it seem routine.

Each of the fleet fired engines to enter translunar injection trajectories. We were on our way, leaving the domain of the Earth and heading for that tiny orb in the distance, the moon. Once we were beyond the Van Allen belts, hard radiation from outer space began to bombard our craft. Each ship had protective shielding, but we still trusted to luck that there would be no solar flares, because that could cause serious problems. Despite all of the moon missions in the last decade, the sun had managed to resist casting a dangerous flare at these mosquitoes which buzzed around its third planet and smaller satellite. One day our luck would fail and we'd be huddled together in the centre of the craft with the heatshield pointed towards the sun, and our fingers well and truly crossed.

Next year, NASA and Roscosmos would be launching two special water-filled, disc-shaped modules which will be towed to shield craft en route to and from the moon.

The two days transit passed quite quickly because most of us were talking about the mission, about each other's lives as astronauts and how exciting it was to be in space. Yes, there was some trepidation about what might be facing us on the surface, but we also felt confident after our intense training at a replica of Moonbase in the Nevada desert.

Soon the main part of the journey was over, and we arrived in lunar orbit. Very slowly and gingerly, each of the spacecraft approached the Gateway. We could see, quite clearly, that there were four Dragonstars attached. The first job would be to detach two of them remotely and park them nearby. That would give us three docking ports to use to berth the three Orions, two Mings and two Uspekhs. As each unloaded its crew, it would be undocked, and Penny would work with the remote operation pilots to collect them all on the end of the Canadarm, Canada's marquee support for all space missions since the shuttle. The Dragonstars could then dock once more ready to take us to the surface. The interiors of all the Dragonstars and each of the Gateway modules were irradiated as we entered just in case LRPs had arrived on the exterior of the Dragonstar we had used for our escape.

'Ming 2 docked,' I heard over the radio and checked it off my list. The two Uspekhs were next and then Orion 2.

'Clear and undock as soon as you're able, Chan,' I said.

'Orion 1, I have you captured,' said Penny who was operating the Canadarm. 'Chi, can you move Ming 1 in beside Orion 1 for me?'

I heard Chi answer in the affirmative.

As we docked and transferred our crews and supplies to the Gateway, we were then undocking and using the mechanical Canadarm to link the craft together using high-tensile cables.

Under normal circumstances there were never more than three or four deep space vessels at the Gateway. Nine ships plus the six Dragonstars being there at the same time was unprecedented. A veritable space fleet. After all the docking had occurred, Anna remotely turned one of the Dragonstars towards the Gateway, backed it off, and took some images of the entire fleet, less that one lander, as they sat silently with the edge of the moon behind them and Earth to its left. Spectacular. Then she brought it in and docked to the Gateway ready for our descent.

The Gateway has a very eccentric orbit, specifically chosen to allow access to many different parts of the moon. In thirty minutes, it would pass directly over Moonbase and we'd get a chance to see if there was any activity on the surface.

'What do you think they might have been doing down there?' asked Bill as we floated to one side of the Russian module with two of their military men, drinking what passed for coffee in orbit.

'That's the great imponderable,' I said. 'I'd imagine they're trying to organise some method of reducing their need for consumables. They'll have worked out that there is only enough food for six months plus whatever they can grow in the bio dome.'

'Could they build a launch vehicle?' asked a Russian captain.

'We think it's more likely that they'll abandon their hosts when food becomes scarce, then conceal themselves in their parasite form until we come looking for them.'

'But for now, they're likely to have retained their hosts?' asked Bill.

'We think so. We hope so, otherwise they might be dead.'

Anna joined us. 'Are you going to contact them or not?'

There'd been fierce debate over whether or not we could negotiate with them. They were obviously intelligent. Could we get them to surrender and allow us to study them?

'Let's see the reaction when we pass over them shortly,' I said. 'They must be observing the Gateway and with all these ships surrounding it, they'll be sure to notice. The question is whether I should radio them to ask them to surrender or wait for an orbit to see if they contact us.'

'I think we should maintain silence,' said Bill. 'Keep 'em guessing.'

'There's no reason to maintain silence,' said Gillian, one of the Marines.

'Why d'you say that?' asked Bill.

'Well, we can't surprise them. Even if we don't make contact first, a fleet of six Dragonstars descending around Moonbase is pretty much a statement of intent,' she said.

‘Yes,’ I said. ‘That’s been the military’s argument all along. The diplomats think we should try it, too, but it has been left for me to make the decision on the spot.’

‘Well?’ asked Anna.

‘I’m going to give them an hour after closest approach with all channels open. Let’s see if they’re going to make contact first,’ I said.

The Gateway had a high-powered camera on the outside of the Russian module. It was linked to a monitor. As the Gateway hurtled towards closest approach, everyone crowded into the ESA international habitation module to watch the screen. Never before had there been twenty-eight astronauts in orbit anywhere, let alone around the moon. Even with the additional CO_2 scrubbers which had been brought by the Russians, systems were operating at their maximum capacity.

‘CO_2 is getting close to limit in here, Mark,’ said Andrei, the senior Russian astronaut.

‘Pay attention,’ I said. ‘CO_2 rising in here. I’m recording the screen. Ten non-military volunteers to go and wait in the Roscosmos habitat. Anyone else – any CO_2 symptoms, leave this module immediately.’ I wanted all the military people to see Moonbase before we descended. We all had photographs and even a model to study, but here was a chance to see if anything had changed. More importantly – had been changed.

‘There it is,’ called Bill.

The camera had been set to maintain the com dome in the centre of the image. We were moving too fast for anyone to manually adjust the camera's direction.

'Can't see any changes,' I said quietly.

'No one outside,' said Pete Hazel who'd been to Moonbase in the past.

'There's a buggy standing near the atmos dome,' I said. 'Wonder why they've left it outside.'

'Yes, odd,' said Pete as the Gateway passed directly overhead. 'Of course, they might not be able to communicate anyway. They destroyed the contents of the com dome, didn't they?'

'Yes, but that was probably because they didn't want any of us reaching out to NASA until we'd been infected,' I said.

'But it could still be out of service.'

'Yes,' I agreed. 'NASA has monitored Moonbase and detected nothing at all. The orbital cameras have also provided images about every forty-eight hours. There's been very little movement detected. The problem is not having continual coverage which might have let us see any trips they've made away from Moonbase.'

'They went to the Chinese habitat, didn't they?' asked Bill.

'Yes, a short while after Linda and I escaped. They stayed for several days then returned to Moonbase. Of course, we don't know if they left anyone in the Chinese habitat.'

Chi added, 'We heard nothing from them while they were there and there's been no answer to any communications from CNSA.'

Moonbase gradually moved towards the horizon of the camera view and eventually vanished. We'd learned nothing.

'Okay,' I said. 'Spread yourselves more evenly throughout the habitats and we'll let the others in here to watch the flyby.'

It was eight pm GMT. I picked up the intercom microphone and said, 'I'm calling them at nine pm. After that, everyone should get the best sleep they can. Tomorrow will be very tiring.'

'Mark,' said Pete over the intercom. 'We have a problem.'

5 Emergency

Pete was remotely manoeuvring Dragonstar 5 to load supplies ready for the morning.

'What's up, Pete?' I asked.

'Dragonstar 5 is misbehaving. I've been trying to dock it onto port seven. It's fine during approach but won't dock.'

I pulled myself through to the communications area and found Pete poring over the remote video feed. 'Look there, Mark. We're approaching, two metres, one and a half, one metre, half a metre…' A minor alarm sounded.

'Every time,' said Pete.

Anna was floating behind me. 'Let me try, Pete.' Anna was our most senior pilot – both Orion and Dragonstar.

She backed Dragonstar 5 away from the port, lined it up again and moved it forward rather more rapidly than had Pete.

The alarm sounded, but the vehicle continued to move forward and we heard a metallic noise as it connected with the port. It appeared to have docked, but the video soon showed that it wasn't secure and was drifting again.

'Pete, can you hold it in that location. I think the only answer to this is to transfer to it and dock manually,' said Anna.

'You want to spacewalk to it?' I asked.

‘Only way,’ she said, then switched communications channel. ‘NASA, Anna here. Need authorisation and support for an EVA to recover Dragonstar 5. It’s developed a fault.’

A couple of seconds later, ‘Okay, Anna, we’ve been watching the failed attempts. Full EVA procedures, please,’ said a NASA voice I didn’t recognise.

‘Dave, can you help me and Penny suit up. Where is Penny?’

‘I’ll find her,’ said Dave and flew through a connecting tunnel to the adjacent module.

Spacewalks always involved two astronauts for health and safety reasons. Odd things could occur when spacewalking and only recently an ISS astronaut had had his helmet completely fog up. None of the usual methods cleared his view and the second astronaut had to bring him back to the airlock. That was fairly easy to recover, but a cut to a suit or some more serious accident would require someone very nearby to act quickly. The protocol of having a minimum of two spacewalkers had been justified.

It took the best part of half an hour to get the two women fully suited up. These weren’t the simple suits we used for short EVAs on the moon, nor the major suits with backpacks for longer lunar operations, but the full EVA suits used from the ISS and for satellite repairs. They were bulky and cumbersome.

Eventually, they were ready. Pete and I moved through to the observation area as they emerged into space. Anna didn't have to fly too far, just about six metres from the Gateway to the Dragonstar. She attached herself to the Dragonstar and Penny detached the Gateway tether and repeated the process so that they were both outside the faulty lander.

Anna opened the hatch.

It instantly jumped to its safety position. This was to protect the person opening the hatch if there was pressure inside. However, it had sufficient force to throw both of the women off the vehicle and give the Dragonstar a vector tangential to the Gateway as the atmosphere within rushed out into space.

Chan shouted, 'It's going to hit Ming 2. Anna, Penny, watch out you don't get crushed.'

I had a good observation spot in the small cupola and could see Dragonstar 5 moving away from the platform. Ming 2 wasn't quite in direct line with its trajectory, but I could see that the two girls were at the full extent of their tethers and, any second they'd be yanked back towards the vehicle. If they were pulled around behind it, in its direction of motion, they could be crushed by any impact between the two craft.

Then bad got worse.

As Penny reached the full extent of her tether, it detached from the Dragonstar. It couldn't have been properly connected, and now Penny was heading off into space in the opposite direction. Of course, Murphy's Law now played its part and, despite the congested space around the Gateway, it looked as if Penny was going to find the only gap between the vehicles and would have nothing to grab hold of or to stop her.

'I'm detached,' said Penny.

'Yes, we see that, Penny,' I said. 'We're following your flight. Remain calm. We'll come after you when we've recovered the Dragonstar. Anna, can you stop yourself being flung around the lander?'

'I don't know, Mark,' she said, remarkably calmly. 'I'm going to hit the side of the vehicle. There are a few places to grab a handhold, but only if I'm the right way around. I'll be doing about seven kph so hoping the suit doesn't get damaged. I'm revolving again.'

Chan said, 'You're still heading towards the section of the Dragonstar to the left of the hatch. I think you'll be face on to it when you make contact, so be ready to grab something.'

'Will do.'

'I think Dragonstar will swipe a glancing blow off the Ming,' said Chan. 'Chi is trying to boot it up to move it to one side. Will keep you informed.'

'Okay.'

'Impact between you and Dragonstar in about ten seconds,' said Chan. 'Dragonstar will impact Ming in fifteen seconds, so you should be safe, but if you can get a handhold, don't let go!'

Chi said, 'Ming powered up. Think I'm too late to move it.'

I saw Anna impact the Dragonstar, and heard several grunts and gasps from her, as she scraped along its hull. On the third attempt, she managed to grab hold of a handrail.

'Warning!' a tinny robotic voice said, reaching us through her helmet microphone. 'Warning! Air pressure falling. Return to ship. Return to ship.'

'Damn it,' Anna said. 'Must have torn something.'

'Anna, are you okay? Can you see any suit damage?' I asked.

'Hold tight!' shouted Chan. 'Impact with Ming imminent.'

'Yes, air escaping from my right arm and right thigh,' said Anna.

I could see the Dragonstar making a slow-motion collision with the Ming. It changed its trajectory and, thankfully, moved away from the Gateway. The Ming came to life and I guessed Chi was directing it back into its original position.

'Report, Anna,' I shouted.

'I'm okay. Making my way to the hatch,' she replied.

'Warning! Air pressure falling. Return to ship now. Return to ship *now*!' said the suit alarm.

I could no longer see the Dragonstar and the next fifteen seconds seemed interminable.

'Inside,' said Anna. A few seconds passed. 'Pressurising. Okay, guys, I'm safe.'

'I don't want that Dragonstar anywhere near Penny. Pete, can you go and get her in one of the others?' I asked.

'Will do, Mark. I'm already suiting up,' said Pete.

'Pete,' called Anna, 'Which one are you taking?'

'Number four,' he replied.

'Could you take number one?' asked Anna. 'That way I can bring number five into number one's port. It's less congested on that side and we might still have problems docking.'

'No problem,' said Pete. 'I'll come back into port seven when I've collected Penny.'

'What's your plan, Pete?' I asked.

'I'll undock, then follow the line of the Gateway. Once I'm past the end I should be able to see Penny. Where is she now?'

'Lost in space,' Penny quipped, belying the seriousness of her situation.

'I'm tracking her okay,' said Chan. 'Range four k and moving at ten kph. Patching coordinates through to Dragonstar 1. I think you'll need them as you won't see her with the moon behind her.'

'Okay, got it,' said Pete.

'Okay,' said Anna. 'About to attempt a manual docking.'

The problem was serious. We needed all of the landers to be able to descend to Moonbase. The Dragonstar began a new automatic approach and stopped when the alarm sounded.

'That's strange, Mark,' said Anna. 'It's not properly aligned. At least five degrees off. Backing off.'

A minute later she said, 'Right, second attempt, but manual.'

I could just see node one from one of the portholes in the European module. I watched Dragonstar 5 begin a second approach. Tiny puffs of propellant issued from various thrusters. The Dragonstar rotated slightly. A few more puffs and it began moving towards the Lunar Orbiting Platform.

I'd done this myself so I knew the procedure. All astronauts had to be able to dock the Dragonstars and Orions in case their pilots were incapacitated, and the automatic systems failed, exactly as was the case here.

I visualised Anna with her hands on the two joysticks. The lander stopped less than half a metre from the docking node.

'Seems fine,' said Anna. 'No alarm. Going for firm dock.'

Someone at NASA said, 'Copy that,' and the lander closed in on the node.

The sound of metal on metal rang through the Gateway, simultaneous with Anna's 'Confirmed light dock. Going for hard dock.'

We couldn't see anything different, but a second or two later, Anna said, 'Hard dock. Powering down.'

'Copy that,' said NASA.

'Well done, Anna,' I said.

Despite all the science fiction films showing people hopping in and out of spacecraft, the reality was that to finish a hard dock required the tightening of a dozen clasps and some integrity tests before she could open the hatch and enter the Gateway. It took the best part of forty-five minutes.

'Approaching Penny. Can you see me, Pen?' said Pete.

'Occasionally. I'm trying to correct a slow spin without depleting SAFER,' she said. 'Was concerned I might need it to get back on my own.'

[SAFER — Simplified Aid For EVA Rescue.]

'Yes, can see you. I'm going to change the approach and come in from above your head.'

'Copy that.'

'I can't see you anymore,' said Pete, who was bringing the hatch side of the Dragonstar towards Penny.

'Okay, can see you above me. Using SAFER jet to stop spin. Hold your position,' said Penny.

Two minutes later she said, 'Right, Pete. I have a firm hold. You sure you depressurised the ship?'

'Absolutely.'

'Right, now tethered. Opening hatch.'

'Copy that.'

'Hatch opened. Pulling myself in,' said Penny.

‘Closing hatch and repressurising,’ said Pete. ‘Then on our way back. The Gateway’s a long way off. More than fifteen k. Looks tiny.’

‘Well done, you guys,’ I said, and I heard a similar comment from NASA.

I made my way through to node one and Anna was emerging from her suit.

‘Torn arm and leg,’ said Chan.

‘Repairable?’ I asked.

‘Yes. We can make temporary repairs, but it’ll need returning to ILC Corp after the expedition,’ said Anna.

‘What happened then?’ I asked.

‘My fault,’ said Chan contritely. ‘I was supposed to depressurise the Dragonstar and didn’t. It isn’t on the usual checklist because we normally enter via the front airlock when in orbit, not the EVA hatch.’

‘Why did Penny break free?’ I asked.

‘I think she was just latching her tether when I opened the hatch,’ said Anna. ‘It must have held until we were jerked back. Thank goodness we have the safety catch on the EVA hatch. If we hadn’t, I’d have been killed by the hatch as it swung open under the internal pressure. Very lucky.’

‘Okay, both of you give NASA a full report. They’ll be pleased that one of their safeguards saved your life, Anna,’ I said. Despite all the care and checklists we have for everything in space, accidents will still happen.

‘What do you think caused the Dragonstar problem?’ I asked Anna.

‘Software. Something was not quite right. Also, there was a sticky thruster and that was stopping alignment. The system got to its pre-firm dock position but couldn’t align. When it applied the thruster, probably nothing happened and so the alarm was sounded. Not enough of a fault to stop us descending, though. Who’s the pilot for number five?’

I checked my tablet and said, ‘Andrei.’

‘He’s very experienced. I’ll talk to him later so he’s aware of it,’ she said and continued to strip out of the EVA suit.

‘What about external damage from the collision?’

‘We’ve asked Pete and Penny to have a look on their way back,’ said Anna. ‘I checked all the systems on the Dragonstar and couldn’t find any additional problems.’

Dragonstar 1 docked nearly an hour later, Pete and Penny having visually checked the outsides of both of the vehicles involved in the collision. We appeared to have been lucky, but it had given us all a shock. Nothing could be taken for granted in space.

6 Descent

I held the microphone a few inches from my mouth and repeated, for the sixth time, 'Calling Ben Lei or Moonbase. Please respond.' Ben Lei was the name of the Chinese habitat which, from lunar orbiter photographs, we knew the infected had visited.

'Calling Moonbase. Please respond. Calling Ben Lei. Please answer,' I repeated, then asked Anna, 'You're sure this is going out on all frequencies?'

'Positive,' she replied.

'They might not be monitoring,' said Pete. 'If there is no one in any of the buggies or in the com dome, they won't know we're calling.'

'Yes, and they're unlikely to have repaired the equipment they smashed in the com dome,' I agreed.

I picked up the intercom. 'No response from Moonbase or Ben Lei. Let's all get to sleep. Eight tomorrow we prepare for the descent.'

I said goodnight to Anna, Bill, Pete and Chi, pulled myself over to the wall and encircled myself with a bungee strap. Most people just attached them to their belts and floated free, but I preferred the security of being held against the wall when sleeping, even if only gently.

I had real trouble sleeping. I kept reliving our escape in the Dragonstar and the smashing of Blake's faceplate as he tried to board us before we could blast off. Then I thought about Linda, who'd been the heroine of our escape. I wished she was with me on this mission. So cool, so competent. I wondered if she were asleep right now, with our child growing in her belly. No, it would be approaching midday in California.

Eventually, sleep crept up on me and the next I knew, my body monitor was sounding its morning alarm.

'Awake!' I responded sleepily, to stop the alarm, then undid the bungee strap and began preparations for the day.

∞∞∞∞∞∞∞∞∞∞

I heard a sharp clunk which told us the Dragonstar had separated from the Gateway.

'Dragonstar 3 reporting separation from the Gateway,' said Anna.

The lagged reply arrived a few seconds later. 'Copy that.'

I heard Penny announce her separation and, seconds later, Chi said that her lander had left the Gateway.

'That sticky thruster is a nuisance,' said Andrei from Dragonstar 5.

'What's up with it now?' asked Anna.

'Once it stuck on. Twice it refused to fire at all, and it came on once without me activating it.'

'That's a bit worrying, Andrei,' said Anna. 'Need to keep a close eye on that as you come in to land.'

'Will do, Anna.'

Through the porthole beside me, in the commander's seat, I could now see all five Dragonstars drifting gradually away from the orbiting Gateway space station.

The view was bizarre, and I took a few photographs as it would be unlikely that such an assembly of craft would all be in such proximity again. 'That's a unique sight,' I said.

'Hope not,' said Anna. 'We're all hoping to come back after this mission.'

'Ah, but not all at the same time,' I said.

She conceded the point.

The view was stunning. The Gateway is a miniature version of the International Space Station in Earth orbit, but most of the modules are attached end to end, allowing plenty of docking stations where each of the segments joined with each other. Six solar panels stuck out of the sides, all tilted towards the sun for maximum illumination. It looked spectacular in the brilliant sunlight.

The ends of the Gateway are called north and south even though they might bear no relation to the moon's poles. The Canadarm stuck out of the south end module of the Gateway although it could walk its way around the space station – both the ends being able to attach to a variety of fixing points. At the end of the arm, I could see an incredible necklace of space craft, an Orion attached by a cable to a Ming, then another Ming, a second Orion, the two Uspekhs and the final Orion. Quite extraordinary.

‘Approaching perihelion,’ said Chi.

‘Ready for lunar orbit injection,’ I said.

‘Copy,’ said Anna, followed by four more acknowledgements from the other Dragonstars.

We all fired at the same time. Although we called it “lunar orbit injection”, it was actually just an adjustment. The Gateway was in a very eccentric orbit because that allowed for more variety of approaches and departures, but we needed to be in a tight orbit for descent to the surface.

‘Fire!’ said Anna.

All of a sudden, the Gateway grew rapidly smaller as we entered our landing orbit. The other Dragonstars maintained their distance from us as if stationary. The Gateway was still receding and was soon too far away to see with the naked eye. All the Dragonstars were on their new orbits. Although we could only see the two behind us, we knew the others were stretched out behind them.

‘Chertovskiy,’ said Andrei. ‘Problem with one of the engines.’

‘Copy that,’ I heard NASA say. ‘Explain.’

‘It’s intermittent and making us spiral. Ah, it’s okay now,’ said Andrei.

‘Copy that. Keep us informed,’ said NASA.

Lunar landing orbit had been achieved, but not faultlessly.

∞∞∞∞∞∞∞∞∞∞

Our tight lunar orbit required us to wait a little over an hour before we began our landing manoeuvre.

'Beginning descent in five,' said Anna.

NASA said, 'Copy that,' but the lag was such that Anna had already fired the descent motor.

The Dragonstar pitched over so that we were now travelling tail first, not the most convenient orientation for viewing the scene. We could both see the surface rushing past beneath us, but we also had television monitors pointing along our direction of travel. Computers were monitoring the distances between the landers. Now was not the time for a collision.

'One minute to pitch over,' said Anna.

I silently counted down the seconds then felt the force of the engines change. We were nearing the surface. The Dragonstar was upright once more. Now Moonbase was clearly visible near the horizon. The navigation had been perfect. Our destination was rapidly approaching.

'Fuel three twenty seconds remaining,' said Anna. 'Is this location okay?'

'What's the range?' I asked.

'Four hundred metres.'

'I'd prefer two fifty or less.'

The motor roared and we pitched forward to prevent any further drop and to move us closer to the domes. The surface skidded by like an escalator beneath us for a few seconds before Anna brought the craft back to vertical and we began to drop

‘Two sixty seconds fuel,’ NASA said.

‘Six metres,’ she announced. Five, three, one, touchdown!’

There was hardly any bump. We were down.

‘Well done, Anna. Perfect,’ I said.

‘Stable landing. Engines off. D3 down, NASA,’ said Anna.

‘Dragonstar 3 down,’ I said over the encrypted radio channel we had with other Dragonstars. ‘Get as close to forty metres to us as possible.’

Four ‘copy that,’ calls came in.

‘Dragonstar 2 down.’

‘D1 down,’ said another pilot over the radio.

‘D5 here. NASA, we’ve got a serious problem,’ said Andrei.

We all knew to keep silent in the case of such an emergency. NASA would respond.

‘Explain, Andrei,’ said Neil.

‘Real problem. Lost stability. Think engine three stopped. Might come down short,’ said the Russian, his voice sounding less than its usual professional calm.

‘Keep reporting,’ said Neil.

‘Sorry. It is firing erratically. Am losing it. Can’t level up. Pitching forward. Can see others landed. Speed increased because angle bad. Trying to turn us north. D2, brace yourselves, we’re coming down close to you! Crew, seal visors!’

‘Avoid them, Andrei,’ said Neil forcefully. The three seconds’ communication delay was a real problem in such a situation.

‘Trying. We’re going to land heavy. Brace! Brace! Brace!’

‘Oh God. He’s going to hit us!’ shouted Chi from Dragonstar 2.

‘Coming in hard! Tipping over!’ said Andrei and shouts could be heard from other members of his crew.

I unstrapped and stood to look out of the port window. D2 was standing about thirty metres from me and I could see D5 descending rapidly at an angle to the vertical.

‘Full power engine one!’ Andrei called.

The Dragonstar made a strange, corkscrew type of manoeuvre which took it past D2. It hit the surface. The forward leg buckled instantly and clouds of regolith were thrown up during the impact. The craft seemed to slide along at an angle, a second leg buckled, and it came down, propped up by the broken legs, at an angle of about thirty degrees, less than ten metres from Dragonstar 2. The whole accident seemed to be in slow motion, an impression enhanced by the regolith cascading back to the surface at one sixth of Earth’s gravity. It was unlike dust kicked up on Earth. There was no atmosphere within which it could swirl. It fell straight down in an extraordinary slow motion. Soon, all movement ended. The scene resembled a still monochrome photograph, the only colour being the scarlet stripes of the flag on the cabin, but even that now had a fine covering of dust, morphing the red into pale rose.

'Crash landed!' shouted Andrei.

'Situation report,' said Neil, urgently.

'A moment,' said Andrei, now a little calmer. 'We've all dropped visors, but no loss of pressure so far. I cut engine a second before we impacted. Fuel gauges show no leaks. Think we lucky. No serious injuries.'

'No fire or smoke?' asked Neil.

'No,' said Andrei, 'but Alexei is complaining of a sprained wrist, though. D5 lying at an angle of twenty-eight degrees to horizontal. Hatch on the right, so no problem exiting. Preparing to leave the craft, in case risk explosion.'

'On our way, Andrei,' I said.

I opened the hatch and Bill Wright was the first to climb down to the surface with two of the Marines and me close on their heels.

Bill stepped off the ladder and said, 'I finally got here.' He looked down at the surface. 'Could any of these things be lying in the dust here?'

'Unlikely,' I said. 'They'd have no idea where we'd land and they are quite small. Shorter than your pinkie.'

'Do you think the infected have watched us land?' asked Doug, the Marine colonel.

'Yes, if they're still here, I'm sure they did,' I said.

The four of us used the strange “bunny hop” gait to approach the stricken Dragonstar. The hatch was open, and the crew were already moving to a safe distance. Alexei was in pain and collapsed into a sitting position.

We joined them. ‘Can’t see any fuel leakage,’ said Andrei, looking back towards his ship. ‘Kicked up a lot of dust.’

‘Yes. Bit of a mess,’ said Anna, who had just joined us.

‘We can’t worry about it now, we’ve a stronghold to storm,’ I said and made my way over to the Marines.

The two Marines were soon joined by others and formed a line between our landing point and Moonbase.

The habitat looked as it always did, a series of shallow- roofed domes nestled together. The main garage dome entrance was directly in front of us and the EVA dome was around to the right. To the left, a long walkway led to the bio dome and we could see the trees and shrubs clearly through the glazed walls. There were no people visible. The buggy which had been standing outside the atmos dome was gone. Further to the left were the fuel and oxygen synthesiser plants and three storage tanks.

We’d rehearsed our plan many times back on Earth and had been discussing the details throughout our voyage. Now we had to put it into action.

With Bill, I stood behind the Marines and swivelled around to make sure everyone was in their designated position.

'Suit still seems very stiff,' said Bill on my personal channel, working his arms around.

'Yes, that's normal. These days we work with a low pressure oxygen/air mixture on the moon, but the suit itself starts the EVA at a higher pressure and gradually reduces it,' I said.

'Why the change?'

'We used to have to pre-breathe oxygen for a couple of hours prior to an EVA to avoid the symptoms of the bends. It did mean we could work at lower psi in pure oxygen, but it was a real bind. Letting the suit control the psi was far better and the only disadvantage was forty or fifty minutes of an overinflated suit at the beginning of the EVA. You'll be down to a lower pressure soon and it'll be much more flexible.'

The ten military personnel with their radiation projectors were standing between us and the domes. Behind me were Andrei and Ludvic, the two Roscosmos pilots; Chi, the Chinese pilot; Anna, Dave and Pete.

Behind them, with the injured Alexei, were Penny, the two nurses, Krishna, the surgeon, and the anaesthetist.

'Do we have a go?' asked Doug.

Satisfied everyone was where they should be, I said, 'Okay, everyone. Follow the plan.' The squad moved forward towards the garage dome, the rest keeping a safe distance. My helmet cam recorded the scene. Twenty-eight astronauts with full EVA backpacks.

7 Map

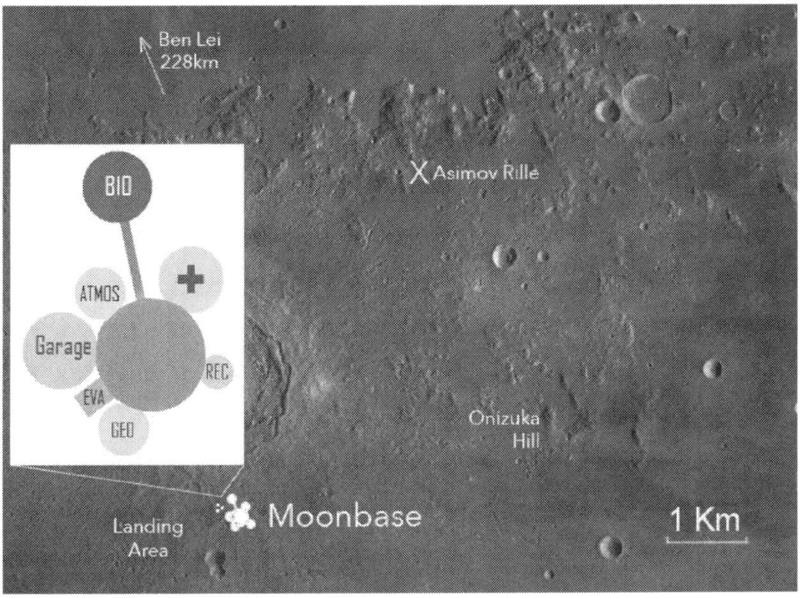

Only the garage dome and EVA dome have access to the lunar surface. Fuel and water storage containers and production plants are twenty metres northwest of the garage dome. The large grey dome contains the com dome, common room, twelve cabins, miscellaneous workrooms and storage areas.

8 Storming Moonbase

'Hold it just here,' said Doug, lifting his hand.

We all stopped. He waved forward and two of the Marines made their way gingerly towards the entrance to the garage dome. One of them was sweeping his or her radiation projector left and right as they progressed. They were looking intently at the ground until they reached the door. The other Marine aimed his projector at the keypad and then swept it up the side of the door, across the top and down the other side. Finally, they both aimed at the bottom of the door.

'Can you check the face of the door too, please?' I asked.

The two figures swept the door as if they were using some sort of paint sprayer.

Doug moved to the door and entered the four digits which had worked the last time I was at Moonbase. No guarantee they would this time, of course.

If we couldn't get in this way, we could still enter via the EVA dome as, for safety reasons, that door could be opened with a simple pressing of a green button. Carbon dioxide build-up in a suit which is running short of air causes the brain to become fuddled. Entry to the main airlock could be a matter of life and death. It would not help to have to remember a number and use a keypad.

'Why did they put a keypad on the garage door?' asked Bill.

'Good question,' I said.

‘Well?’

‘No idea. You’ll need to ask Neil. Perhaps they were worried about neighbours borrowing tools.’

Bill laughed.

‘No,’ said Anna. ‘You need a keypad so that the computer knows someone is wanting to enter. It could then give a warning to anyone working in the garage to either suit up or leave.’

‘Ah. All is now clear,’ said Bill.

I watched as Doug pressed his helmet against the door. A few seconds later he said, ‘I can hear the air recycler running. Should open as soon as the atmosphere nears zero.’

‘Good news,’ I said. We wanted to get in this way as it would allow everyone to get inside quickly. The EVA dome airlock was too small for a crowd of twenty-eight astronauts.

It is strange observing events on the moon. The lack of sound gives the impression it is all part of a silent movie. The instant the door began to rise, a Marine irradiated the bottom of the doorway in case anything was lurking inside. There was the usual disturbance of the dust as the last of the atmosphere blew outwards as the door opened. It was almost impossible to reduce a pressurised space to the vacuum outside so there was always an outflow.

‘More dust outflow than normal,’ I said.

‘Why would that be?’ asked Doug.

'The LRPs might not have been keeping the garage as clean as we usually did,' I said.

'So, nothing sinister in it?'

'No, Doug. Wouldn't have thought so.'

The door continued to rise. The Marines had taken up positions either side of the door and the rest of us kept our distance. There were no guns at Moonbase, except for Blake's illicit air pistol which we had played with occasionally in the rec dome. Nevertheless, the infected were perfectly capable of building some sort of projectile-firing device or grenade. We didn't think they would, though. They'd probably want us alive.

It was an anti-climax. The door was fully open, and the garage appeared to be deserted.

'Marines enter!' said Doug. 'Spread out and irradiate as you go. Don't forget the ceilings.'

The squad moved forward. Bill and I followed them in.

'No buggies,' I said.

'There are two buggies over there,' said Bill, pointing to the refurbished and improved Apollo XVI buggy and a second more sophisticated open vehicle.'

'Yes. I meant the larger enclosed buggies. Computer, where are the crew?'

There was no reply.

'Computer, please respond. This is Mark Noble.' Again, there was no answer. It must be off-line.

'Wonder where the main buggies have gone,' I said. 'Neil, the three buggies are gone. They've only left the open vehicles. Is there a recent picture of the Ben Lei base? Could they be there?'

After the usual two second delay we heard Neil say, 'We'll check, Mark. I'll get back to you. The one at your and Linda's blast-off location hasn't moved. We know they went to Ben Lei, but returned.'

'Okay, thanks. Could someone also check the lunar reconnaissance orbiter to see if buggy tracks can be seen running elsewhere? I assumed they would be in the garage. Two buggies would tear up the regolith substantially and the tracks should be visible.'

'Copy that, Mark. We're on it,' replied Neil.

'Mark, we've finished our search. The garage appears to be clean,' said Doug.

'Okay, the rest of you, come on in,' I said. 'Anna, Pete, you both know the garage form. Can you clean up the dust? Doesn't look as if it has been done since Linda and I escaped. Drop the door when we're all in, please, Bill.'

'Will do.'

I made my way over to Doug and the other Marines who were keeping the door from the garage dome to the main dome under surveillance.

'You're ready?' I asked.

'If there is anyone behind the door they'll be quickly irradiated,' said Doug. 'Our only real concern is a projectile or grenade attack and that would be less likely to hurt us once the atmosphere is reinstated.'

The door was now sealed, and I could feel the atmosphere climbing, allowing the suit to collapse around my body instead of being blown up in imitation of the Michelin man. As soon as the atmosphere reached 0.8 of Earth, the inner door could be opened from either side. Eighty per cent is a perfectly workable environment and puts less stress on the joins between building segments. Anyone living above six thousand feet is experiencing 0.8 of an atmosphere, so there is little effect on the human body. All of us, of course, had been tested for susceptibility to altitude sickness.

'No one open their visors yet. I want the entire base checked first,' I said.

A green light appeared above the door, meaning that pressure on each side was equal.

'Anna, Pete, can you cut the vacuums until we've checked the main passage?' Doug asked.

I heard the cleaning machines stop. The place was silent but for the continual background whirr of the air circulation pumps.

'Okay, Everyone keep clear. Open the door,' said Doug.

The interior doors were also extremely secure as they were protecting the interior of Moonbase from vacuum, if the garage were open to the surface. Gradually it slid to one side, revealing an empty corridor stretching almost the entire width of the main dome.

'Nothing,' said Bill.

'B-squad, with me,' said Doug, 'clear the main corridor.'

Four Marines moved along irradiating floors, walls and ceilings. Bill and I followed at a safe distance. Doug stopped at a door on the left and beckoned us closer. It was the entrance to the medical centre.

'This door is badly damaged,' Doug said.

'Yes. We'd sealed it to keep the infected in the medical bay, but they'd broken out,' I said and I crossed the passage to look through the oval glass panels in the doors to the com dome. 'Better check medical and the com dome first.'

'Will do,' said Doug, and I heard his chatter as he called more military personnel forward to tackle and irradiate those areas.

At the end of the corridor, adjacent to the passage to the rec dome, was the entrance to my cabin. Next to the com dome door was another double door to the common room. I peered inside and it looked pretty normal, apart from a lot of dirty plates and utensils lying around. It looked as if the infected were not particularly fastidious when it came to housekeeping.

'Medical clear,' said Mike, the Marine captain, emerging back into the corridor.

‘Common room now, Mike,’ said Doug. He opened the door.

What a fright I got when I had Doug’s clearance to enter the common room! Commander Blake Smith’s putrefying corpse was sitting upright at his desk, staring at me as if he was a zombie awaiting the opportunity to rise and attack. I was glad my visor was still in position. It didn’t look as if he would smell too pleasant.

I watched Doug irradiate him, while the others checked the rest of the room.

Gillian and her team arrived in the common room, ‘Com dome clear. Oh my God! Is that one of the crew?’

‘Yes, Blake, the commander,’ I said.

She composed herself then reported, ‘The com dome equipment is less badly damaged than it appears. Superficial mainly. The consoles are wrecked but the electronics seem almost intact,’ she said.

‘That’s odd,’ said Bill.

‘Well, not necessarily,’ I said. ‘The infected might not have realised that the innards of communication devices were more important than the consoles themselves. Remember that the LRPs were only interested in us not being able to communicate with Earth.’

‘Sorry,’ said Gillian. ‘I didn’t mean any of it is usable, but much of it could certainly be recovered. Zoya and Mikhail are going to get started on repairs after they’ve checked the remaining domes. How do we get into personal cabins?’

‘We need the computer up and running. Currently it is not responding. Penny and Dave are working on it,’ I said.

No sooner had I said that than I heard the computer say, ‘Recovering systems and data.’ Then a minute later, ‘Rebooting.’

We continued to hear various announcements as different systems were brought into play. Once the reboot was complete, it announced, ‘I recognise that Peter and Anna are here, not on Earth. The only active crew member is Mark. Instructions, please. What has been happening?’

‘Good afternoon, computer. Are all systems running?’ I asked.

‘Yes, Mark. All systems are running, but I cannot locate Blake, Mary, John, Linda, Roy, Jenny or Crystal. Can you provide their locations?’

‘NASA override code two, two, six, delta, alpha, nine,’ I said.

‘I recognise you as the new Moonbase commander, Mark.’

‘Blake is dead. Linda is on Earth. We do not know the locations of Mary, John, Roy, Jenny or Crystal. Anna is my deputy commander. Acknowledge.’

‘Acknowledged, Mark. What has occurred? Who are the people I do not recognise?’

‘I think you were switched off some time ago. An entity called the Lunar Regolith Parasite, or LRP, has possessed the bodies and minds of the missing crew. Each of the squad who are here will give their details to you at the common room terminal. Are all systems operational and unlikely to fail in the next month?'

'Checking,' said the computer.

Meanwhile, all the military not on sentry duty had congregated in the common room.

'All areas clear, including storerooms,' said Doug. 'We just need access to crew quarters.'

'Shortly,' I said.

'All Moonbase systems operational, Mark. No data coming from buggies one, two or three. Cosmic ray detectors appear to be disconnected,' said the computer.

'Doug, get a couple of your guys to bag Blake and put him in the cold store off the surgery,' I said.

'Sure thing,' he said.

I walked over to the physical computer terminal and keyed in a security code.

'Computer. You recognise that code?'

'Yes, Mark. I recognise that code.'

'Doug, are your Marines ready at each cabin door?' I asked.

'Ready, Mark,' he replied.

'Unlock all crew cabins.'

'All crew cabins unlocked, Mark.'

I called across to Doug, 'That's the cabins open, Doug. Report back when they've all been checked.'

'Will do,' he said.

I turned to Penny and Dave who were awaiting instructions. 'The bio dome's been checked. Will you two make sure the hens have food? If they've been scavenging, they will have lost condition. Collect all the eggs you can find and put them in the incubator in the bio dome office. Some will possibly be fertile, but we can't eat them because we have no idea when they were laid. Also check the irrigation is functioning normally.'

I called Neil using the radio we'd brought with us. 'Any news on the buggies?'

After the usual delay, 'The LRO (Lunar Reconnaissance Orbiter) is passing over Ben Lei in about forty minutes and we'll get back to you, Mark.'

When Penny, Dave and the Marines returned, we all felt a little easier. Except for the security detail, we had removed our suits and were enjoying a meal.

At least Moonbase was secure and had plenty of supplies, but where were the five remaining infected crew and the LRPs? I had expected traps and ambushes, but there had been nothing.

9 Stocktaking

'They're not at Ben Lei,' said Neil. 'We'd been watching it anyway, but the latest pass shows nothing there.'

'Thanks, Neil. Have you sent that detailed local image yet?'

'Should be with you any second.'

The printer sprang into life and like a pot that takes forever to boil, the image gradually emerged from the printer's mouth, a millimetre at a time.

Once complete, I grabbed it and a magnifying glass and sat at one of the dining tables. Bill brought us both a coffee and sat down with me.

'What are you looking for?' he asked.

'Unusual clusters of tracks,' I said to him. 'Computer, is that orbital tracking system running yet?'

'Spasmodically, Mark. But only buggy three is showing within the current tracking distance.'

'Computer, is it still at the launch site east of Moonbase?'

'Yes, Mark.'

'I wonder if the Marines can roll it into an upright position,' I said to Bill.

'What does it weigh?'

'Computer, what's the weight of a buggy?'

'The six-wheel buggies have a specification of four thousand pounds empty, Mark.'

‘What would that be on the moon, computer?’

‘Six hundred and sixty-six pounds, Mark.’

‘Doug,’ I called, and beckoned him over. ‘Do you think your Marines could roll a buggy over? Weighs about two tons on Earth but less than eight hundred pounds here,’ I said, making a mental allowance for buggy three carrying some stores.

‘I’m sure we could,’ he said confidently.

‘Right. Get Pete to help you fire up the open buggies in the garage. Take as many men as they’ll carry. You’ll have to travel about four miles to where buggy three is located. Pete will drive it back. He’s experienced with them. Anyone can drive the open buggies with a bit of trial and error.’

‘Okay. Will do, as soon as we’ve finished here,’ Doug said.

I peered at the aerial photograph again.

‘There’s a lot of track activity between here and Asimov Rille,’ I said, pointing out the darker marks of the tracks to Bill.

‘Yes, I see.’

‘Neil, come in please,’ I said.

A slightly longer delay this time. ‘Copy, Mark.’

‘Can you check the orbiter’s most recent images of Asimov Rille, to the northeast of Moonbase? There are a *lot* of tracks leading that way.’

‘Copy that,’ said Neil.

‘What is the Asimov Rille?’ asked Bill. ‘Sounds interesting with a name like that.’

‘Yes, it is. Roy and I were scheduled to do some work there after we’d returned from our crater survey,’ I said. ‘There are lots of rilles on the moon. Most are collapsed and show as no more than grooves in the lunar surface, but the Asimov Rille is much smaller and appears to be intact. They’re caused by volcanic activity in the moon’s distant past. Lava once flowed out of these tunnels. They exist on both Mars and the moon and could offer readymade shelters to combine with above surface bases like Moonbase.’

‘Could they be hiding there? Surely not?’

‘It would seem unlikely, Bill, but they must be somewhere. Why didn’t they lie in wait for us? They couldn’t know about the radiation projectors.’

‘They seem very intelligent, Mark. They might have assumed we’d come up with a way of dealing with them or we wouldn’t be here. I think we should likewise assume they’d have had some plan in place.’

‘Yes, worrying. We need to keep evaluating their strategic options,’ I said.

‘How long could a rille tunnel be?’ asked Bill.

‘Could be extensive. Apollo 15 landed near Hadley Rille. It was huge, but most of it had collapsed. Some others are thought to be intact,’ I said.

Penny came over with Dave and handed me a tablet. Penny said, 'That's the inventory comparison with the computer's running list of stocks, Mark.'

'Any large discrepancies?'

'Yes, there're three pages of them,' said Dave. 'Strange that first item.'

I was shocked at the extent of the list.

- Replacement EVA airlock x 1
- Two metre square aluminium sheets x 6
- Microscope x 1
- Container of spare medical equipment x 1
- Three metre lengths of steel channelling x8
- Sealant guns x 3 (used to seal air leaks) plus six refills
- Three metre aluminium ladder x 2
- Microwave x 1
- Camp beds x 6
- Bundle of bedding materials x 2
- Kettle x 1
- Acid gun x 1 (used to break down the sealant) plus two refills
- Ten metre roll of opaque cloth x 1
- Self-contained toilet x 2
- Cooktop (hob)
- Shower cubicle and base with fittings x 1
- Case of cosmic ray detector spare parts
- Replacement oven
- Quantum particle detector

- Case of spare parts for the quantum particle detector
- Pick x 1
- Spade x 2
- Five hundred mil silicone tubes x 8
- Nitrogen cylinders x 6
- Oxygen cylinders x 8
- Hydrogen power generator x 1
- Hand operated excavator x 1
- Carbon dioxide scrubbers x 2
- Box of medical consumables x 1, containing gloves, wipes, tissues and so on.
- Cartridges for scrubbers x 12
- Coffee machine
- Gurney x 1

The list continued into another two pages.

'What the hell are they building?' I asked in astonishment.

'It couldn't just be that the previous stocktake was wrong?' asked Penny.

'Well, I did the garage and main stores myself a day or so before we had to flee, so I know most of that will be correct. Why the airlock?'

'Looks like they're building their own base somewhere,' Bill said. 'They couldn't make a ship out of that, could they?'

'No,' I agreed. 'A habitat is certainly a possibility. Penny, send the list to Neil and see what he makes of it. The more I study it, the more it looks like a habitat.'

'Mark. You copy?' said Neil.

'Yes, copy you.'

'Good guess, Mark,' said Neil. 'There are two buggies standing at Asimov Rille and the regolith is churned up substantially at the tunnel entrance.'

'Penny's sending you the inventory shortages. We think they must be building a habitat. Most of the food is gone, too, so, wherever they are, they are supplied for at least three months. Much longer if they are rationing,' I said. 'By the way, I've sent the Marines to recover buggy three.'

'Okay, copy that. We'll look at the inventory laterally in case there is something offensive they could be doing with it. Assume you're all keeping suits on or close?'

'Yes, lightweight suits, Neil, except for some of the military. As soon as the Marines are back, we'll be calling for a sleep period with four on guard,' I said.

'Copy that. We're looking at that lost inventory now. How are the communications repairs progressing?'

'Copy that, Neil. Repairs ongoing. I'll keep you advised.'

At that moment, Penny entered the room in a state of some agitation.

'What's up, Penny?' I asked.

‘NASA asked for readings from the quantum particle detector as part of catching up on missing data since Moonbase was evacuated,’ she said.

‘And?’

‘No readings were stored in the database, nor raw files. I decided to go and look at the detector and took Ivan with me. It’s gone!’

‘What do you mean, gone?’ I asked, wondering why anyone would want the particle detector.

‘It has been very carefully disassembled and removed. Not like the smashing of equipment in the com dome. This was specifically dismantled and taken away,’ she said.

‘Okay, add it to the list of missing stores and check other equipment packages outside the domes,’ I said.

‘The alpha magnetic spectrometer is also gone from the experimental platform. Including its cooling system. Very neatly dismantled,’ said Penny.

‘There are quantum and other particle detector spare parts missing too, Mark,’ said Dave. ‘They’re on the list.’

‘Yes, and both smaller spectrometers are missing from the top of the atmosdome,’ said Penny.

‘Yes, puzzling. Seems like they have a real interest in particle physics. Curiouser and curiouser,’ I said.

‘And the rille might be the rabbit hole!’ said Penny.

I turned to the others, 'Okay. I want everyone breakfasting at seven GMT. You'll ensure a four person guard overnight when you get back, Doug.'

'Sure thing, Mark,' he said, and went off to organise the expedition. We needed an enclosed buggy. Buggy three was the one Linda and I had used to escape the infected crew.

'Andrei, can you and Chi go and have a look at your Dragonstar. Chi will be able to ascertain if it's something we can repair in our machine shop or whether it needs more specialist equipment. Take a couple of Chinese and Russian Marines with you. Enjoy the excursion… and keep your eyes peeled,' I said.

'Chi wants to get over to the Ben Lei base to see whether there are any of them there and to check their stocks and equipment,' said Andrei.

'No, it is not a priority. It'll have to wait until we have all the buggies back in service, so not now.'

'She was talking about hopping over there with Dragonstar 2,' said Andrei.

'Yes, good idea, but not until we're finished here and have made some progress finding the LRPs,' I said.

'Okay, I'll let her know. We'll get over to Dragonstar 5 and assess the damage,' said Andrei and went to find the others.

10 Transport

Colonel Doug Baker and his Marines entered the garage dome. Pete Hazel, who had previously had a gig at Moonbase, went straight over to the two open buggies and began routine checks to ensure they were ready for the trip to recover buggy three.

'How many will they hold, Pete?' asked Doug.

'You're restricted to three on the Apollo buggy, but the other one could hold four or five if we drive carefully.'

'Okay. Dave, you, Gillian and Vicky on the Apollo buggy. Danny, you and John with me and Pete on the other one. Get properly suited. Full gear and grab a couple of projectors. Check they're fully charged,' said Doug.

'Both buggies ready to go,' said Pete.

'Show Gillian how to use the Apollo.'

About thirty minutes later, the door was open, and Pete watched as Gillian tentatively guided the Apollo buggy through the doors. It waited outside while Vicky positioned herself on the small floor area behind the two seats.

Pete drove the larger Moonbase buggy out of the garage. There was no problem getting three passengers on board.

'Computer,' Pete said over the radio, 'close the garage doors.'

'Garage dome doors closing, Pete.'

Pete kept his buggy behind and to one side of Gillian's as they made their way towards the more remote Dragonstar take-off location. Over to the right they could see Andrei's team walking towards the fleet of Dragonstars. Number five stood at a rakish angle on the surface.

'My goodness, it didn't miss number two by much. Will they be able to fix it, Pete?' asked Doug.

'What, Dragonstar 5's legs? Possibly. It depends whether we can rebuild the leg in the garage, then it will just be a matter of lifting it upright. Once we've sorted buggy three, we can attach the Moonbase Canadarm to it and use that for leverage.'

'I'm amazed how well organised you are here, Pete.'

'When you're a quarter of a million miles from the nearest service station, it pays to have a well-equipped workshop.'

The two buggies gradually covered the distance to the original Dragonstar launch site. Both of the open machines were labouring under the unusual amount of weight they were carrying with the extra passengers.

Soon, in the distance, buggy three could be seen. It was lying on its side with the door open and facing upwards. That wasn't good. Dust would possibly have been thrown into the cabin from the Dragonstar lift-off.

Once they were twenty metres from the machine, Doug called a halt and asked two of the Marines to approach the buggy, sweeping their irradiation from side to side across the regolith.

'Okay, now walk all the way around it, irradiating it. Don't miss any areas,' said Doug.

A few minutes later, 'Done, sir.'

'John, climb onto it. Irradiate the entrance thoroughly.'

The suited figure jumped onto one of the wheels, took hold of a stanchion and hauled himself onto the top. He sat astride the main body and irradiated the entrance, the door and the visible part of the cabin.

'Done, sir. Shall I enter?'

'Vicky, join John on top of the machine. Then you can enter with John and do a full sweep of the interior,' said Doug.

The suited figure was seen to lower himself into the interior with Vicky peering inside after him. They heard John say, 'Computer. Interior lights please.'

'Lights on inside,' said Vicky.

Suddenly, there was a shout from John. 'Bugs, we've got bugs in here!'

'Get inside, Vicky, and irradiate John,' said Doug, and the second figure disappeared from view.

A minute later, John reported, 'All clear, sir. Four dead bugs.'

'We've irradiated the entire interior three times, sir,' said Vicky.

‘Okay. We’re coming in,’ said Doug and the other Marines approached the fallen buggy.

‘Damaged wheel,’ said Pete.

‘Will it stop us using it?’ asked Doug.

‘No. It’ll get us back to Moonbase and we can change the wheel there. No damage to the axle.’

Doug and Pete climbed onto the body of the buggy and lowered themselves into the interior.

Everything was disarranged, of course. The seats in the front section were sideways on and anything loose on the port side of the vehicle had fallen onto the temporary floor which was the starboard interior wall.

‘Where are they?’ asked Doug.

‘Here,’ said Vicky, passing him a food bowl.

In the bottom lay four of the LRPs, gradually fading from clear gel to cloudy after death.

‘Give me that projector,’ said Doug, and John handed over his weapon.

Doug irradiated the inside of the bowl from above, for at least a minute, then handed the projector back. ‘Where were they?’ he asked, looking up at the hatchway and port wall which was currently the ceiling.

‘As I dropped into the buggy, I saw one fall onto my right arm and another onto my faceplate. The one on my arm tried to get through the glove seal. I irradiated it and it fell off me. As Vicky dropped in, I saw another drop onto her and we irradiated each other,’ said John.

'So, they were hiding?' asked Pete.

'Andrei, are you hearing this?' asked Doug.

'Yes, Doug. We've just completed irradiating Dragonstar 5. Seemed sensible after hearing what you encountered over there. All clear here and no sign of any LRPs,' said Andrei.

'And is the damage repairable?' asked Pete.

'Looks possible,' said Chi. 'One leg is a wreck, but there doesn't appear to be any damage to the jets or integrity of the craft. We can build a new leg. Once that's done, we'll need to find out why Andrei lost a descent jet.'

'That won't be so easy,' said Andrei. 'We're heading back with the broken leg and landing plate after we've checked each of the other Dragonstars and set a couple of traps for our friends. Just simple bits of tape to show whether doors have been opened.'

'Yes, good idea, Andrei. Especially so as we are now certain they're trying to attack us,' said Doug. 'Great care when you get back to Moonbase. No hitchhikers!'

'Damn right,' said Andrei.

'Okay,' said Doug. 'Everyone out of here. Let's see if we can roll this thing over. John, last one out shut the hatch. If it rolls too far, we don't want it to be damaged.'

Soon, all seven were standing on the surface, looking towards the top of buggy three.

'Right,' said Doug. 'Take a firm hold then wait for my command on four.'

The Marines astronauts planted their feet firmly in regolith and gripped their designated lifting points – mainly parts of the starboard roof rack structure.

'One, two, three, *lift!*'

The buggy, in moon's one-sixth gravity, rose remarkably quickly. After it reached about thirty degrees, the Marines could not lift it further until they changed holding points. Three were able to keep it in position. The other four took hold of rails along the line where the cabin joined the chassis.

'Firm hold, you four?' asked Doug. There were several affirmatives. 'The rest of you, take your new handholds and, on four – one, two, three, *lift!*'

The buggy passed its centre of gravity and swung upright, then began to fall to port, before rebounding. The motion dampers came into play and it was upright and motionless in just a few seconds.

Pete climbed the ladder to the hatch and climbed inside. He sat in the left commander's seat and said, 'Cavor, how much power remaining? Full systems check, also.'

'Certainly, Pete,' said the buggy's computer. 'Power is at twenty per cent. Systems check underway.'

'Doug, we've plenty of power to get us back to Moonbase. Suggest four of you join me leaving one on each open buggy,' said Pete.

'How about that damaged wheel, Pete?' asked Doug.

‘Shouldn’t cause a problem. We can change it back at Moonbase. Benefit of having six wheels.’

‘Moonbase, Doug calling.’

There was a short delay before Anna replied, ‘Yes, Doug.’

‘We’re on our way back.’

‘Great. Full irradiation of everything before you open the garage door. Same with your group, Andrei,’ said Anna.

‘Copy that, Anna. We’ll be on our way shortly,’ said Andrei.

Anna looked at me and said, ‘Everything seems to be going rather too well.’

‘Yes,’ I agreed. ‘Let’s keep alert. Still can’t figure why we didn’t find a reception committee. Even more so now that we know some were waiting in buggy three.’

‘One buggy safely recovered,’ said Doug when he found me in the common room. ‘The offside rear wheel was damaged, and Pete is showing the Marines how to change it.’

‘Well done. How did it go?’ I asked.

‘Those open buggies are fun when they’re not overloaded. I drove one back on my own. Brilliant. They do a fair lick.’

I laughed. ‘Yes, over thirty mph. The Apollo buggy a little less,’ I said.

‘The buggy was easier to turn over than we expected,’ said Doug. ‘The batteries, tools and chassis are quite heavy, so the centre of gravity was low. The suspension also allowed seven of us to lift the main body. Once it reached about sixty degrees, the whole thing just sprang into the upright position.’

‘Yes, good design.’

‘Here’s the dead LRPs,’ Doug said, handing over a sampler containing the milky white slug-like pieces of gel. At least it proves the projectors work.’

‘Yes, good we were prepared. I think you should all get some sleep now. I’m calling an eight hour rest period as soon as Andrei’s back. You’ll set up a guard? One person in each area.’

‘Yes, will do, Mark. How will the infected be dealing with supplies of water and air?’

‘Water can be extracted from the regolith in deeper craters. As they have taken the spare water extractor that won’t be a problem for them. They took a quantity of air and can make oxygen out of the regolith too,’ I said.

‘They’re better equipped than I expected. Buggy three had a lot of dust in it. I’ve got three guys vacuuming right now. I’ll call Andrei and get him to leave the leg outside and come in through the EVA dome to save disturbing the work in the garage.’

‘Can’t help thinking they must be planning something. Strange none of them were in Moonbase,’ I said.

It was almost two hours later that Andrei's team returned to the safety of Moonbase and the rest period could begin.

So far, there had been no sign of the LRPs. A CT scan had shown that Blake's body was not infected, confirming that they could escape after death.

What trap were they laying for us at Asimov Rille?

Whatever it was, we'd find out tomorrow.

11 Visitors

On the moon, daylight lasts fourteen Earth days, and so do the nights. Moonbase crews always use Greenwich Mean Time to keep some semblance of normal sleep, relaxation and work periods. Crystal knew this which meant that her LRP did too.

The EVA airlock, when opened from outside the dome, usually ran a pump to cycle the air back into the main facility. The pump could be heard throughout the Moonbase corridors and in rooms adjacent to its housing. The sound would be enough to alert any guards on duty. Crystal was using an emergency valve to allow the air to vent into space, from the dome to the moon. If done slowly it was almost silent. It took much longer, and it seemed an age before the red light flicked over to green. The black woman's face inside the helmet looked at the door opening mechanism. The change of light colour meant that there was vacuum inside the EVA dome.

Crystal swung over the safety lever and turned the spigot-like control which unsealed the door. She did everything slowly and quietly, knowing that noises could travel through the building itself, even if silent in the vacuum of space.

Her gloved hand grasped the handle and she pulled. Initially there was a little resistance, then the silicone seal released its grip and the door opened. Roy joined her at the door and the two infected astronauts entered the dome.

Very slowly, and as stealthily as possible, Crystal closed the outer door and sealed it, and Roy pressed the large green button on the inner wall which allowed air to fill the dome from the general Moonbase supply. Unlike the garage dome, the small EVA dome did not need pumps to pressurise, so repressurisation was almost silent. One minute later it matched Moonbase.

Roy wiped the glazed section of the inner airlock door which had developed some misting from the humidity in the atmosphere of the main dome. He peered into the corridor. One space-suited person was sitting about fifteen metres along the main corridor looking at a handheld tablet. Roy watched him or her for a while and saw the regular movements of the fingers of the right hand which indicated that the person was changing pages, so probably reading an ebook.

Crystal took a sampling container from a pouch on her hip. It was about twenty-five centimetres long and maybe ten in diameter. She unscrewed the lid.

Roy cracked open the door, stopping and looking at the guard. No movement. He opened it a little further and checked again. Still no movement. He repeated the process until the door was open about twelve centimetres. Still no movement from the guard.

Crystal dropped to her knees and placed the open cylinder into the gap. Forty almost invisible transparent LRPs were quickly out of it and rapidly climbing the walls of the central corridor, their movement a cross between a jet-propelled slug and a supercharged inchworm. They concealed themselves beside light fittings and electrical trunking.

Roy pulled the door closed and sealed it.

Crystal walked to the other end of the EVA dome and turned the spigot which allowed the air in the dome to leach out into the vacuum of space very slowly, again avoiding the use of the pump. Their suits began to swell as the pressure dropped.

Soon the door was open. Crystal closed the spigot and they both left the dome. Together, they sealed the airlock, closed the outer spigot and pressed the repressurise button. They waited until the red light came on to indicate that the dome was repressurising, then made their way back to buggy two which was sitting, facing away from Moonbase, ready to go.

As if in a silent movie, the space-age buggy drove away from Moonbase towards the Asimov Rille.

Inside Moonbase, fully aware of how to control human beings, one LRP was already climbing the guard's back. It knew there would be one dangerous moment. When it slithered over the lip of the faceplate it would be visible. It readied itself. The guard, Gillian, clicked to turn the page of the ebook.

Whether or not, for a moment, she saw the LRP, there was still no time to react. In an instant, it was on her cheek, through her skin, controlling the central nervous system and paralysing her.

Gillian jerked and twisted on the seat. The Kindle clattered to the floor and then it was over. The LRP, now in control, reached down and collected the ereader.

Another guard appeared beside her. 'You okay? Heard a noise.'

'Nodded off and dropped my Kindle,' she said.

'Boring this.'

'Yes.'

'Going to get a coffee. Want one?'

'Good idea. Might wake me up.'

Mikhail turned towards the common room. Four LRPs hitchhiked on his suit.

12 Infiltrated

It was ten in the evening in California, but only six in the morning at Moonbase. I was just finishing a Skype call with Linda and she was very well. The bump still wasn't visible. I missed her and despite the infuriating communication delay, I'd enjoyed seeing and speaking to her.

'I was thinking,' she said as I was contemplating ending the call to get ready for the day.

'Miracle! Fire away,' I replied.

'It was about the fact there was no one there. That they'd all gone off somewhere. I started wondering why.'

'They realised we must be prepared to tackle them in some way, so they vamoosed,' I said.

'Don't underestimate them, Mark. I wouldn't have done that.'

'What, you wouldn't have left?'

She sat quietly. The communication delay was frustrating. The view behind her showed the illuminated night-time cityscape from the apartment window. She linked her hands together. 'No. We know they are very intelligent. What if they are outthinking you?'

'In what way?' I said. Knowing how bright Linda was, anything she said would be useful. Again, the few seconds delay was enforced by the limited speed of light.

'I'd have come back after you'd checked the domes and caught you unawares!'

God, she was right. We hadn't thought about them coming back to attack us.

I pressed my personal intercom button and asked, 'Computer, when was any exterior door last opened?'

'At oh five twenty hours, Mark.'

'What? Are you sure?'

'I am certain, Mark.'

'Who went out?'

'No one, Mark.'

'Who opened the door?'

'Crystal, Mark.'

'What the fuck! Crystal? Was anyone with her?'

'Roy was with her, Mark.'

'Christ! Computer, what did they do?'

'They stayed for a few minutes, opened the inner airlock, but never entered the main corridor. Then they closed it and left.'

'You've got a problem,' said Linda. 'I'll hang up. Be careful.'

'Bye, darling. I'll call you later,' I said, and the screen returned to my desktop view.

'Computer, where are Anna, Bill and Doug?' I said.

'Anna and Doug are in their cabins. Bill is in the geo dome, Mark.'

I quickly pulled on the airtight gloves for the lightweight suit I was now wearing, closed the visor, took a small irradiating projector and opened the door cautiously. I could see a guard sitting in the corridor, reading. It looked like Gillian, but there was no one else.

I reached Doug's cabin, the door opened and I was face to face with him. I lifted my finger to my lips in the age-old sign for silence and pointed into his cabin. He backed in and stood beside the desk.

'Doug. Do exactly what I say. It is important. Put your hands in your pockets,' I said.

He looked at me with a puzzled expression and did what he was told. I leaned forward and peered into his eyes. They looked perfectly normal. No sign of the blank expression the LRP gave the infected.

'Stand still. Don't move,' I said, then I lifted the projector, squeezed the trigger and irradiated him. 'Who are you?'

'Marine Colonel Doug Baker,' he said, crisply.

'Sorry about that, Doug. I had to check.'

'What's going on?'

'We've been infiltrated.'

'Seriously? When?'

'Just after five this morning.'

'Ah the time of maximum drowsiness,' he said.

'Two of the infected got in through the EVA dome and I think they must have released LRPs,' I said. 'Suit up, quick.'

I pressed my intercom button, 'Hey, Bill, you about?'

'Yep. Geo dome. Couldn't sleep. This damn daylight. I was looking up information on that rille.'

'Wait there, will you? I'll come through.'

Doug was suited up, grabbed one of the larger projector weapons and the two of us made our way, quickly, out of his cabin. We knocked on Anna's door, carried out the same tests and the three of us continued down a side corridor and into the geo dome, checking no one was concealed along the way.

Inside, Bill was sitting on a tall stool at one of the benches studying a map and the computer screen. We checked for anyone else concealed inside either side of the entrance and walked over towards him.

'Bill. Do exactly what I say. Stand up, turn around, hands in pockets and face us.'

'What?' he said as he rose. 'Oh, hi, Doug, Anna. What's going on?'

'Stand still,' said Doug, making it clear the projector was pointed at him.

I stared into his face. 'All clear. We've been infiltrated, overnight.'

'How?'

I explained what had occurred and we discussed how we were going to proceed. Our biggest problem was not knowing how many had been affected.

'Computer, where is Krishna?'

'He is in the surgery, Mark.'

‘Computer, is anyone else in the surgery?’

‘Alexei and both nurses, Jack and Diana, Mark.’

Bill closed his faceplate and we all left the geo dome. There was still just the one guard sitting in the corridor. We approached her; it was Gillian.

‘Hello, Gillian, all quiet?’ I asked.

She was about to answer when Doug irradiated her with his weapon, and she collapsed to the floor.

‘Quick, carry her into the surgery,’ I said, and we headed for the medical dome.

I opened the double doors cautiously. Three of the four strong medical team were sleeping on makeshift couches. They woke as we entered.

‘Can you all stand and face us, please? Where’s Diana?’ I said.

‘Sleeping in ward A. What wrong with Gillian?’ asked Alexei with his clipped English.

‘Just stand still and face us. Hands in pockets!’ said Doug, rather more forcefully than I would have.

We checked their eyes.

‘We’ve been attacked. Gillian has been infected. We’ve dosed her. Can you do a full body scan and be sure not to allow skin to skin contact with any of you? She might contain several LRPs, so a really thorough check, please. Doug is going to irradiate you and the room lightly to be sure you’re not carrying any of them on your person or clothing. Someone wake Diana.’

‘Poor Gillian,’ said Alexei and Jack as they took her from Doug and Bill and began to strip her out of the spacesuit.

‘Let’s hope I can keyhole it out of her,’ said Krishna.

‘Bill, Anna, stay here with projectors,’ I said pointing at them on the shelf nearby. ‘You guard them until we get back.’

‘Will do. At least we now know for certain that the projectors work when a person has been infected,’ said Bill.

‘Keep a close eye on the doorframe. If there are live bugs around, they’ll be able to get in through the damaged door without much of a problem,’ I said, feeling most relieved that none of them had already been infected.

‘Doug, where’s the emergency multidirectional projector?’ I asked.

‘Damn it. It’s in the common room, still in its packaging.’

‘Not good. Exactly where? I don’t recall seeing it. Why’s it not set up?’ I said, trying to control my anger at this oversight.

‘A tall cardboard box between the left end of the kitchen counter and the lounge area. I was going to set it up this morning. When we realised Moonbase was not occupied it dropped in priority. Sorry, Mark.’

‘It’s still sealed?’ I snapped my question.

‘Taped, yes.’

'Okay, let's be methodical about this,' I said. 'Computer, how many people are in the common room?'

'There are eight people in the common room, Mark.'

'How many in the com dome?'

'There are nine people in the com dome, Mark.'

People had put makeshift bunks in common areas. I wondered how many were awake. 'Where are the rest, computer?'

'In the bio dome and the surgery, Mark.'

'Right, Doug, let's check out the rest of medical.'

Doug and I checked the two wards and cold store for anyone hiding, then made our way out in the main corridor. Doug walked one way up the corridor irradiating, while I did the opposite direction.

Eight crew in the surgery were clear and one being treated. There were still another nineteen to check. How many LRPs had they released into Moonbase? They would almost certainly have moved into the common room. We were in trouble.

'Common room next, Doug?'

'Think so.'

'How do we do this?' I asked, bowing to his superior military knowledge as a Marine colonel.

'I'll head in first. You follow and be ready to irradiate me with the larger projector if I'm attacked. Then we'll irradiate the others and see how many collapse. While I'm doing that, can you open the multidirectional projector and hit the red button on top? The on-switch is right beside the red button.'

'Okay, ready when you are,' I said.

Doug approached the common room door.

13 Fear

Doug barged into the common room and surveyed the scene. It only took a second or two to see who was where.

Dave Flowers, Jimmy Stott and Penny Heston were sitting at a table on the right apparently taking an early breakfast, Penny turned around as Doug entered.

Ai Zhao, Lucy Li and Zoya Indlikova were at the kitchen work surface talking. Mikhail Deskov was studying one of the food storage lockers.

Where was the eighth? The moment Doug realised the shortfall, Vlad Melsovic charged at him from behind the door.

The doors were swinging shut, but I caught sight of Doug being floored by the large Russian and his small projector skidded off across the floor, spinning as it went.

I rushed into the room with my larger projector already on, pointing it at Vlad as I entered. The Russian collapsed on top of Doug. At the same instant, I saw a lump of clear jelly fall onto my arm and another onto my faceplate. In addition, Mikhail was running towards me from the counter and Dave, Jimmy and Penny were rising from their table.

For an instant I was stationary, mesmerised by the LRP which was trying to squeeze its way past the seal on my glove. The other one was rapidly crossing my faceplate to get at the seal where the helmet joined the shoulder assembly.

In a flash, I realised that the large portable projectors were not designed to turn on oneself, it would be no good to me, only the multidirectional projector could help before this thing was inside my suit. I swung to the left, managing to irradiate Dave and Penny as I did so. The cardboard box containing the multidirectional projector was by the window in the lounge area. I ran flat-out towards it across the non-skid floor which helped prevent low gravity accidents.

Almost as if in slow motion I saw Jimmy change his direction towards me and Ai, Lucy and Zoya dropped their utensils and started along the same vector.

It was going to be a near thing. I sprayed the three women, but the range was too great, only one stumbled. I threw the projector at Jimmy, catching him square in the face and slowing him down. Only six metres to the box.

I tried to brush the LRP off my arm, but it got a grip on my other glove and was now trying to get in through the left-hand seal. The one on my helmet had vanished. I guessed it was at the neck-join and trying to squeeze itself through that seal. We knew from my experience in the Orion that they could reduce themselves to microns in width. The seal would not protect me for long. Only three metres.

Jimmy threw himself at me in a rugby tackle, didn't get the best of grips and I managed to kick myself free. One metre.

Zoya was going to get to me as I reached the carton. It stood a metre high and about half a metre square. I punched my left fist into the cardboard, simultaneously noticing that the LRP was almost into my glove, then I twisted to the right to knock Zoya onto the floor with a body check.

With one hand in the top of the carton, I pulled myself around and felt for the on switch. Thank God it was on my side of the machine. I flicked it on, felt a searing pain in my left wrist and slammed my right hand down onto the raised button.

The pain was horrendous and I felt sick. I fell onto my side and looked around. Mustn't pass out. My wrist felt as if a stream of boiling water was falling onto it. Doug was leaning over me when I gave up the struggle and passed out.

14 Theatre

Slowly, in a mental haze, I regained consciousness. I was lying on a gurney in the medical centre. Krishna, the surgeon, and Diana, one of the nurses, were peering down at me. I felt woozy. God, my wrist was sore.

'Ah, back in the land of the living you are,' said Krishna.

'What on Earth is wrong with my wrist?' I asked as I looked down at the bandaging and splint to hold my left hand in line with my arm. Had I broken it somehow?

'We've given you morphine,' Krishna said. 'The LRP was entering your body as you fired the multidirectional projector. It died and changed back to its original shape, tearing the skin and flesh at the entry point. That would explain the pain.'

'But I'm clear?'

'Yes, but I'd like you to sleep or, at least, lie still for a couple of hours. Then we'll look at how necessary the splint is.'

'I need to get up to date!' I said, forcefully, trying to sit up but falling back with my head spinning. 'Is Anna, Bill or Doug about?'

'Doug's on his way from the bio dome,' said Krishna. The door swung open. 'Ah, here he is now.'

'You're okay, Mark?' Doug asked.

'Yes. Bit disorientated. Fill me in.'

'You hit the button just in time. The bug was halfway into my glove.'

'It worked then?'

'Yes, sure did. I am so annoyed with myself for not setting it up earlier. Stupid mistake,' said Doug.

'We are where we are. What's the situation with the people?'

Krishna said, 'The eight in the common room are all up and about. All the LRPs were dead, close to the outside of the skull and we managed to get them with keyhole surgery.'

'What's the recovery time?' I asked, worrying that we would be severely understrength.

'Only two or three hours. Once the headache's gone most are back to normal. One or two are still suffering and I've signed them off until tomorrow. Gillian was not as lucky, though. We have her in ward one and will operate later to remove it. It is inside the brain tissue and might have caused some damage.'

'Not good,' I said.

'No, but it could have been worse. She is conscious, but has a hell of a headache,' said Doug.

'I remember the feeling,' I said, casting my mind back to Wilmington Hospital.

'We'll get it out,' said Krishna.

'And the others? What happened?'

‘I dashed over here and Bill and I rushed the com dome,’ said Doug. ‘Got them all. Their tactic relied on surprise. We were lucky. Another fifteen minutes and they’d have infected everyone. The med team has already dealt with victims. No problems.’

‘And the three in the bio dome?’

‘Ah, interesting. When we entered, we immediately irradiated John Dyson and Dave Morgan, then we heard Vicky Jones calling for us not to shoot. She was down one of the aisles. I irradiated a section of the dome near the main door, got her to stand in it and Bill kept the projector on her while I went around the entire dome irradiating all the plants, chicken coop, ceilings, the office and paths. One of the chickens passed out. Don’t know if that was an experimental infection.’

‘They infected a chicken?’

‘Think so,’ said Doug.

‘Vicky gave herself up?’ I asked.

‘Yes, it did. We mustn’t forget that it is one of them. It is no longer Vicky. We got it to strip out of its clothes, irradiated them too, and let it dress again. Completely clear. We’ve been holding it in the bio dome office waiting for your recovery.’

‘Why didn’t you just irradiate her?’

‘Well, it must know where the others are and what they’re doing in the Asimov Rille. That seems pretty valuable intel,’ said Doug.

‘Yes, I’m not thinking clearly. Hold her until Krishna releases me. We’ll tackle her then. You’re sure there are no other LRPs in Moonbase?’

‘Absolutely, Mark. We used the multidirectional projector in each open area. If there are any more, they’re in the bio dome office with Vicky. I have two Marines on guard with the brief to irradiate the door every ten minutes. It’s not a foolproof strategy, but it will do for a while.’

‘And further attacks?’

‘We now have exterior two-person patrols using one of the open buggies to circle Moonbase on a continual basis. When power gets low, they switch buggies. We also have a permanent two-person guard at each entry point plus pairs at two locations in the central corridor so that the entire length is covered,’ said Doug.

‘How’s the com dome?’ I asked.

‘Dave Morgan says it should be fully operational by tomorrow afternoon, but not all of the communication equipment will be fully operational for up to a week.’

‘That’s enough, I think,’ said Krishna. ‘Sleep you must.’

∞∞∞∞∞∞∞∞∞∞∞∞

By the afternoon I was almost fully recovered. My wrist was extremely sore, but I could survive with ordinary dressings.

When I thought about what had happened, I was annoyed at Doug not setting up patrols from the start and not unpacking the multidirectional projector immediately. It seemed sloppy to me. If it hadn't been for Linda voicing her concerns, we could all have been infected. Doug had realised his mistake and apologised. Was that enough?

Later, Anna, Bill, Doug and I made our way down the tunnel into the bio dome. Inside, Mikhail and Zoya were on guard outside the office. They were both seated. Zoya to the left of the door and Mikhail seated about three metres away facing her. The smaller projectors had a range of about four metres. We could see Vicky sitting inside the office.

Mikhail and Zoya stood as we entered. Doug briefly irradiated each of them.

'There might be free bugs inside the office by now, of course,' said Doug.

'Okay. Get her out and check,' I said.

Mikhail opened the door, told Vicky to leave the office and sit in his seat. Zoya kept her covered while Mikhail did a thorough job of irradiating the entire office and the doorway.

The four of us stood a couple of metres away from her and she regarded us coldly.

'We know what you are,' I said. 'Presumably you realise we can kill you with these.' I lifted a projector.

She didn't answer.

'What are you doing in the Asimov Rille?' asked Anna.

The LRP in Vicky turned her gaze to my second in command but said nothing.

'If you're not going to talk to us, we might as well kill you. If you give us useful information, we could let you leave your host,' I said.

'And why would you do that? You would never let me roam free,' said the LRP.

'Better death for you than captivity, then?' I said.

'Killing comes easily to you. So far you have killed many of us. Are you not interested in discovering another intelligent species? Is that not one of NASA's prime scientific objectives?' it asked.

'But when you take us over, you suppress our minds. It isn't a symbiosis you're seeking, but total domination,' I said.

Anna surprised me by asking, 'Can you release Vicky and let us speak to her?'

'I can, but how would you know if it was her or me?'

'An interesting question. Let her speak to us,' I said.

Vicky's body slumped in the chair, then recovered and looked around at us. 'What's happening? One of them got me.'

'Vicky, what's 238 plus 162?' I asked.

She immediately replied, '401.'

Her body twisted in the seat and sat upright. Her eyes glazed and she spoke again, 'That's wrong. It's 400.'

‘Yes, we are aware of that and all of our people know a number of special responses if asked particular questions once they were infected,’ I said.

‘I am not an infection. I am a living being,’ it said.

‘You are a parasite. You are imprisoning and torturing your host. I *know*. I experienced it,’ I said.

‘We can work in symbiosis too and have been doing so in the Rille.’

‘Do not harm Vicky. We’ll consider what we might do with you,’ I said and then to the colonel, ‘Lock her up again.’

‘Mikhail, Zoya, get her back into the office then irradiate the seat and area surrounding it,’ said Doug.

The four of us left the bio dome and headed back to the common room where we hit the multidirectional projector button to ensure we’d not brought any passengers.

‘So, the host is inside and can be released,’ I said.

‘What if it had learned about the question from Vicky and had known to add the digit to that question?’ said Doug.

‘Possible, but I do think we were definitely talking to Vicky. I looked carefully at her eyes and they’d lost that glazed expression we always see in the infected,’ Anne said.

‘Yes. I’m sure it was her as well,’ I added.

‘So, what do we do?’ asked Bill.

‘I don’t know,’ I said. ‘Does it take us forward? Is it any real help at all?’

‘It had a point,’ said Anne. ‘We’ve not only found alien life, but also intelligent alien life. That’s rather remarkable and the first thing we do is kill them.’

‘But they can take us over. It’s too dangerous to have any sort of relationship with them,’ said Doug. ‘The whole point of us being here is to destroy them.’

‘We’re putting off the inevitable,’ I said. ‘We need to find out what is going on in the Asimov Rille. Is buggy three operational?’

‘Yes,’ said Anne. ‘Wheel replaced and cleared of dust. Took some time. That regolith gets everywhere.’

‘Yes,’ I agreed. ‘Buzz Aldrin, in his book, said that the biggest problem with living on the moon would be the regolith. He was dead right. It’s so invasive.’

‘He didn’t know about the bugs when he wrote that,’ said Doug.

I chuckled. ‘True. I want you, Pete and two Marines ready to leave at nine in the morning. Anna, you’ll command Moonbase while I’m away. Now, I want a conference with Neil,’ I said, and we all left the bio dome.

Talking to Vicky and knowing she could be freed by the LRP was a new development. I needed to know what Earth thought about it.

15 Reconnaissance

Anna, Doug, Bill, Pete and I spent nearly two hours suffering the irritating three or four second delay between each question and answer. Finally, we settled on saying "over" at the end of each sentence, but it still wasn't easy as we all wanted to break in on each other from time to time. Frankly, I was glad when it was finished and looked forward to a good night's sleep and an early start.

The Marines had done a great job cleaning out buggy three. It looked almost new inside and not a speck of dust remained after its ordeal, lying on its side at the Dragonstar launch site.

We had four small projectors and two of the larger ones with us. We also were wearing full pressure suits rather than the less substantial and more flexible moon expedition outfits. After the experience Doug and I had had with the LRPs gaining access via the gloves, I felt more comfortable with the hard seals on the EVA suits. We knew the LRPs, given time, could get through them, but it would offer what could be a lifesaving delay. Bill was staying with Anna to provide support. I made a mental note to get him trained on the buggies as he would be more useful to me than Pete.

The garage dome door lifted, and I gently steered us out onto the surface. Doug sat beside me and Pete shared the rear with two Marines, Mikhail Deskov and Ivan Volkov. In the mirror, I saw the door closing behind us. To my left, the Apollo buggy was coming into view as another two of the Marines continued their circular patrol of the habitat.

During my first stint at Moonbase with my geology buddy, Roy, we'd had the buggy to ourselves and driving over the surface of the moon had seemed surreal. We'd both had trouble fully absorbing that we were actually on Earth's satellite and that no one had ever driven here. We'd rarely covered the same ground twice, so it was literally virgin regolith. The buggies churned up the dust and the tracks were darker once the surface was broken. It would not be possible to avoid being tracked if anyone had a mind to do it. It was a huge privilege to be working and living on that tiny orb in the sky we'd seen all our lives from Earth.

My thoughts were broken by Doug, saying, 'Still can't believe I'm really here and that it is the moon, the real moon, spread out around us.'

Maybe everyone feels the same. I laughed, then said, 'I was just thinking about that. Roy and I used to discuss the impossibility of where we were regularly while we were driving.'

From behind us, Pete said, 'I feel exactly the same and I was in Moonbase for a whole eight months. You never quite get used to the enormity of it. I still love to sit by the window in the common room, staring out at that incredible vista.'

'Yes, us too,' said Mikhail, and Ivan nodded.

'How far to the rille?' asked Doug.

‘Only about eight miles, but I’m taking us in a wide sweep so that we can approach face-on to the opening. It’ll also mean we’re coming from an unexpected direction.’

Unless driving at speed, the suspension of the buggies was superb and it gave a smooth ride. The front section where there were two seats, also had large windows allowing us to see a considerable distance in all forward directions.

To my left were moon mountains standing over two thousand metres high, yet they had unexpectedly gentle rounded slopes. Artists’ impressions prior to 1969 always showed jagged peaks. It was only after the Apollo 11 landing that we discovered they were more like rolling hills. To the right was a similar range though not so high. Those mountains were far enough away that we couldn’t see their bases. The moon’s horizon was only a mile and a half away, so most of the mountains on the right were hidden from view. We were only seeing their convex summits. The basin floor before us, although this was not a well-worn route, was relatively smooth. I steered around larger craters, only driving over those small enough not to give us too uncomfortable a journey.

Silence accompanied us as we continued to be amazed at the scene before us. Driving across the moon… breathtaking!

‘You think they’ll be waiting for us?’ asked Doug.

'Yes. By now they'll know their invasion of Moonbase failed and this must be our next move. See the hill dead ahead?'

'Yes.'

'The rille is just to its right. It'll be visible in about half a mile,' I said, cutting the speed to about five miles per hour. 'We know the plan, so just keep the options and possibilities we discussed in your minds. Nothing usually happens the way you think it will, so we must also prepare for anything.'

'Is that it?' asked Doug, pointing at a slight rise with a dark shape in its centre. Two buggies stood to the right of the entrance.

I cut the speed to three miles per hour. 'Hmm. Expected them to have put the airlock at the entrance. Shows how you can never be sure of anything.'

I slowed to a stop about fifty metres from the cave entrance. 'Okay. Let's go see. Pete, you stay here and be ready to react if we need you.'

'Sure thing, Mark,' he said.

Doug and I moved into the rear section of the buggy. Pete moved into the cockpit and lowered the airtight transparent wall between the cockpit and us. We could now get in and out without needing to repressurise.

'Everyone sealed?' asked Doug.

We all answered in the affirmative.

'Cavor, reduce air pressure to zero in the aft compartment, please,' I said.

'Pressure reducing, Mark,' said Cavor, the on-board computer.

'Ha, is that a pet name?' asked Doug.

'No. All the buggy computers were named after characters from *The First Men in the Moon*. Cavor, Selena and Bedford, although Selena wasn't actually in the cast. That name is based on Selenite, the name H G Wells used for the moon people,' I said.

'Never heard of it,' said Doug.

'It was good fun. Look it up, especially as what we are about to do with this rille fits in nicely with Wells' plot. Descending into caves beneath the surface.'

'Pressure zero, Mark,' said Cavor.

'Right, open up, Mikhail, then the two of you get out and look lively on the surface. Keep your eyes peeled,' said Doug.

Exiting a buggy was not as simple as leaving a car. The hatch had to be opened outwards and backwards to where it connected with a clip. The astronaut then backs out of the hatch, trying to find the top rung of the ladder with his feet. Then it becomes rather more straightforward and he climbs down the ladder onto the surface.

Mikhail was first out and removed his projector from where it was attached to the side of his backpack. Ivan lowered the two larger projectors down to Mikhail who moved a couple of metres away to allow Ivan to climb down. Doug and I followed and the four of us looked towards the rille.

The surface here was relatively normal. Plenty of pockmarks had been left by impacting meteors. Nothing huge, the biggest maybe two metres across. The lip rose ten to twelve centimetres above the surface and the depth was similar. This one had a central peak which rose to, maybe, twenty centimetres higher than the mean. Most had no central peaks. Apart from four or five close together, over to our left, there were only ten or so between us and the rille.

In front of the rille, the surface had been seriously churned up and we assumed this had been done by the buggies and the unloading of the considerable amount of material the LRPs had filched from Moonbase.

The entrance to the rille was a cave mouth set into the slope of the hill. It was about three metres in diameter. It faced south so we could see a fair way inside. Examination of photographs from the Lunar Reconnaissance Orbiter showed that the land behind the entrance rose to about ten metres and continued some way before blending into the surrounding raised ground. From above there had been no sign of the rille collapsing and so we had to assume the tunnel continued for some distance. It had just a single entrance or they'd have needed more airlocks, and there should be no direction from where we could be caught by surprise. Pete would monitor our backs from the buggy.

'Now, remember,' said Doug, 'we don't irradiate anything or anyone unless it is a matter of personal safety. Keep an eye on each other's suits for any bugs. You know what they look like. Shout out if you see one.'

Doug began to walk slowly towards the cave with me at his side. Mikhail and Ivan flanked us.

We stopped at about twenty metres. Still no sign of LRPs or their hosts. Buggies one and two stood to the right of the cave mouth with their hatches closed. They had no lights and there was no sign of any movement.

'We could take the buggies and head back to Moonbase, then return with a larger force,' said Doug.

'An option, but not yet,' I said.

Three minutes later we were at the mouth of the rille. I shone a powerful LED torch into the cave, scanning the ceiling and walls, looking for the glint of any LRPs. Nothing!

'Okay,' I said, 'inside.'

'Mikhail, Ivan, you follow us at a distance of three metres,' said Doug. 'Keep playing your lights over the backs of our suits and helmets as well as the ceilings and walls.'

'Why not irradiate as we go?' asked Ivan.

'After the event with Vicky, yesterday, I spoke to NASA and we're hoping they might want to communicate,' I said.

We'd walked three metres into the cave and stopped as Ivan shouted, 'There! Look!'

We all turned to the area he was indicating. Four LRPs were sliding along the wall deeper into the rille. We quickly, and not particularly calmly, shone our torches all over the cave around, above and below us. There were just those four.

'Don't shoot,' said Doug. 'but keep your torch on them so that they know we are aware of them.'

No others appeared, but two of them rushed ahead, moving like supercharged slugs and we soon lost sight of them.

'They must be rushing to tell the others,' said Doug.

'Yes, possibly,' I agreed.

The other two continued to move deeper into the cave at the same speed as us. They could easily match our walking speed and it was no problem to follow them. We were now about fifteen metres into the rille. I kept looking behind us, checking we were not somehow being cut off.

'Wait,' I said a few metres later. I was becoming increasingly concerned about being ambushed.

'Mikhail, can you make your way back to the cave entrance using your torch to thoroughly scan the floor, ceilings and walls.'

'Yes, sir.'

'What're you thinking?' asked Doug.

'I want to know if any trap is being set for us. Mikhail, let us know if you see *anything* move,' I said.

'Will do,' he said and began to make his way back towards the entrance. We could see his torch beam circling the cave in front of him.

'Sir. Those two bugs seem to have stopped,' said Ivan.

He was right. They were sitting on the wall, about three metres ahead of us, seemingly waiting for us to continue.

'Anything, Mikhail?' Doug asked as he saw Mikhail stop at the cave entrance.'

'Nothing.'

'Return to us, Mikhail,' said Doug.

'They could block our retreat with the buggies,' I said.

'Wait there for a minute, Mikhail. Pete. Can you hear me?' asked Doug.

'Copy you, Doug,' said Pete.

'Any sign of any movement of the buggies?' Doug asked.

'No. No movement.'

'Doug,' I said. 'I'm tempted to go back and check the buggies are empty so that we can be certain we won't be trapped in here.'

The cave seemed to go on much further. The torches didn't show any features other than the rippled walls, roof and floor.

'Okay,' said Doug. 'Ivan, you and Mikhail check the buggies for any sign of one of the LRP's hosts. Report back. We'll wait here. *Don't* irradiate any bugs you find inside them.'

I shone my torch onto the two LRPs. They seemed to be stationary, waiting for us to make the next move.

'Doug, scan the rest of the cave around us. I don't like this situation,' I said.

I kept my beam focused on the LRPs and became aware of Doug's torchlight moving over the rest of the cave.

'Nothing, Mark. They're pretty easy to see on this darker rock in here,' said Doug.

'Volcanic,' I said.

The two LRPs hadn't moved since we'd stopped progressing.

'Suit check!' said Pete.

We checked our O_2, power and cooling systems and each reported no problem. This was something we needed to do every thirty minutes. It was routine for EVAs on the moon.

Mikhail said, 'I'm in the hatchway of buggy one. No one in here, but I can see a bug on the water container. Can't see any others. I'll descend so Ivan can check I've not picked up any passengers. What do you want done with the bug?'

'Nothing,' I said, 'but shine your torch on it to make sure it knows you have seen it and have done nothing.'

'Done that,' said Mikhail. 'Now leaving the buggy.'

Ivan said, 'Mikhail's clear. Buggy one hatch closed. Moving to buggy two.'

They carried out the same examination and, again, found just a single LRP inside.

'We've both exited. What now?' asked Ivan.

'Catch up with us,' said Doug.

We waited in the spooky interior of the rille, always keeping the LRPs in sight, until the lights of Mikhail and Ivan approached.

Doug pointed onwards and we continued along the cave into the gloom. Our gelatinous hosts kept pace with us, leading the way. We made slow progress. There was another suit check, so that was an hour gone.

'What's this ahead?' asked Doug, quietly.

All but Ivan swung our torches forward along the passage, while he kept the two LRPs in his beam.

'A junction,' I said. 'That's a surprise!'

'Why?' asked Doug.

'It means that two separate lava flows met here. Explains the larger space at this location,' I said.

'The left one slopes downwards gently, while the right one descends much more steeply. Which one?' said Doug.

'The LRPs are taking the left branch,' I said.

'Mikhail, Ivan, take the right branch, great care, walk down looking for anything which could endanger us,' said Doug, then to me, 'I'm still concerned about being cut off.'

'Yes,' I acknowledged. 'I don't like this, Doug. We're isolated from safety and down to four hours power and air.'

'We can get back more quickly than we've been walking in. Half hour max,' said Doug.

'Entities, can you hear me?' I asked, in case they were listening to our radio.

'They can't hear us. We're on the scrambled channel. Select channel four to be open,' said Doug.

The radio controls were located beneath my helmet on the left side. I used the mirror on my glove to let me see and I selected channel four. 'Entities, can you hear me?'

The Marines returned and told us they'd seen nothing to suggest that the steep sloping passage was in use and, at that moment I heard, 'I can hear you.'

16 Voice In The Tunnel

'My name is Mark. Who am I speaking to?' I asked.

'Roy Williams.' God, it was my geology buddy.

'Can we meet, Roy?'

'You're killing us. How can we trust you?'

'We've the same problem. You dominate us if you touch us,' I said.

'We've learned to work with our hosts. We're no longer a threat.'

'But you made a major assault on us yesterday during our sleep period,' I said.

'Yes, we thought it would be easier to explain if we were inside your minds. We realise it was a mistake and now we don't know how best to proceed to correct matters,' said Roy's voice.

'Then let's meet and talk. We have already spoken with one of you in Moonbase. We know you can free the host,' I said.

'Will you give us safe passage if we come to Moonbase?'

'Why not here and now?' I asked.

'If we invited you inside, you could kill us all. We don't have a defence against your radiation beams. We're very vulnerable. We're only protected by the airlock and the rock surrounding us.'

'I could give our word,' I said.

'Not good enough. We're mourning over forty of our kind. You've killed that many of us and we don't know what orders you have had from NASA. Following orders might overrule your word. We can't take that chance, but two of us will come to Moonbase to discuss matters if you guarantee safe passage.'

'Only if you do not bring any more entities with you. We will provide safe passage for two of you to discuss the situation.'

'Return to Moonbase. Two of us will follow for a meeting,' said Roy's voice.

'What are you doing at the rille?' I asked.

'We'll discuss it at Moonbase. We are placing a lot of trust in you as you can easily kill us with your beams. My host says I can trust you, but I'm wary.'

'You can trust me. I promise. Allow an hour for us to prepare an area in Moonbase for the conference,' I said.

Was Roy still alive and sharing his body with this LRP? If we got him back to Moonbase, even if the talks went badly, we could soon kill his entity and I'd have my great friend back to normal. I felt guilty thinking along such lines. I'd given my word, but these things were a nightmare.

'You still monitoring the two LRPs?' asked Doug on the secure channel.

Mikhail confirmed he was. 'No change, just waiting.'

'Okay, Roy, we're returning to Moonbase. Allow an hour before following,' I said.

‘We’ll allow an hour,’ said the LRP housed in Roy’s body.

We turned around in the tunnel and made our way towards the entrance, through which we could see the brilliant light of the lunar day. I must admit to being greatly relieved once we had left the cave.

∞∞∞∞∞∞∞∞∞∞∞∞

‘Buggy approaching,’ said Pete Hazel as he stood with Mike Robertson in the garage dome, looking out of the raised door. Two more Marines equipped with large projectors had taken up positions either side of the entrance. They all wore full pressure suits.

‘Copy that, Pete,’ I said from the geo dome where we’d set up the facilities for the secure meeting. We were having to record the session for NASA as we still had no high bandwidth connection to Earth from anywhere but the com dome.

The geo dome was the main laboratory for the bulk of moon research. The usual lab benches would allow three or four people to work with Bunsen burners, taps and sinks, microscopes, electron microscope, and all the equipment which might be found in a modern chemistry laboratory on Earth. In an area near the door, we had set up a table and a number of chairs for the first ever official meeting with alien intelligences. I had to keep reminding myself that this was not a meeting with some sort of rebel human alliance, but with bona fide alien creatures.

‘Roy. Do you copy me?’ I asked.

‘Yes, Mark.’

‘When you enter the dome, you are to disembark and stand clear of the buggy. We intend to irradiate it to ensure you have not arrived with more entities.’

‘I understand,’ said the LRP who was using Roy.

We could see the interior of the garage dome on a monitor and watched buggy one enter and stop about five metres from the door, which began to close.

A few minutes later, when pressure had equalised, Roy and Crystal got out of the buggy, in lightweight helmetless pressure suits. They stood at the foot of the ladder and the Marines signalled them to move a few metres away from the buggy.

‘Mark,’ said Mike, ‘there is a bug on Roy’s shoulder, in full view.’

‘It is one of us and is normally in the buggy,’ said Roy. ‘Do not harm it. I’ve brought it out with me to ensure its safety.’

‘Okay, Mike. Leave it be. Irradiate the rest of the buggy,’ I said.

‘Wait,’ said Roy. ‘I’d like more distance between us and your beams. We’re too close.’

We watched the Marines as they allowed the alien delegation to move further away from the vehicle.

‘Far enough?’ asked Pete as the infected humans moved about five metres away from the buggy.

'This will be a sufficient distance,' said Roy. Somehow, they had worked out the range of the projectors. How had they done that?

One of the Marines began sweeping his projector over the outside of the buggy and followed that with comprehensive inside irradiation. 'All clear,' he said.

The inside door of the garage dome opened and Anna entered. With Mike, she collected the visitors and followed them into Moonbase, keeping them covered with small projectors. The geo dome door opened, and they all walked into the conference area.

Four Marines were standing guard against opposite walls. I sat with Bill Wright on one side of the table with a seat for Anna. Roy and Crystal would sit opposite us where Vicky Jones, the other infected astronaut also sat. Mike Robertson moved over to stand by two of the Marine guards. To their right was the multidirectional projector, our security blanket. In an instant we could kill all LRPs within the room.

They looked so ordinary. Roy had grown a beard. Crystal's ebony skin contrasted with the white of the suit. I looked into their eyes and saw the slight blankness of their stare.

Before sitting, Roy offered his hand to me.

'If you don't mind, I'd rather not touch your skin at this time,' I said. 'If this is going to be meaningful, we need to be talking to your hosts, not their entities.'

Roy sat. His head remained still, but I could see his eyes become brighter and clearer. 'This is me, Mark,' he said.

The eyes had certainly changed and were full of life.

'Okay, explain why we should not irradiate you. Tell us why you prefer to keep the parasite rather than rid yourself of it. All you need to do is say, "Do it," and we'll clear you right now.'

'No, Mark. You mustn't. You gave your word. I have grown to know the entity within me, and we work together far more effectively than alone. Apparently, we're old friends from the dawn of humankind on Earth.'

This fitted in with what we knew about the creatures. They were similar looking to the hippocampi we already had in our brains. I wanted to hear their perspective on it. 'Explain,' I said.

'The entities don't know their origin,' said Roy, 'but the one inside me, the first of them, believes he was dormant in the regolith for millions of years. He thinks that vast hordes of them passed through the solar system. He was unfortunate enough to land on the moon. Most landed on Earth. They entered animals on Earth and discovered that they could work well with most mammals, improving their survival rates. Inside humans they were able to develop intelligence and improve memory, all of which helped animals develop and become more efficient hunters.'

‘But our hippocampi,’ Anna said, ‘don’t suddenly decide to jump ship and infect other people. They are part of us.’

‘It wasn’t always like that. At some point in the distant past on Earth, the entities must have become part of the animals they inhabited and were then already present in the brains of their hosts at birth. My entity doesn’t know how or when that happened. It would take much research on Earth, to discover the biological processes behind it. The fact it happened fascinates him and, to be fair, me too.’

I looked at his eyes again. ‘You’re saying that we owe our human faculties and abilities to them?’

‘Exactly,’ he said.

This was definitely Roy speaking, unless they’d found a way to stop the glazed expression. ‘So what benefit is it to you, Roy?’

‘My vision is clearer. I can control bodily functions better, slowing my heart when sleeping. My mathematics, logic and dexterity are much improved, and he gives me total recall of everything I have ever seen or learned,’ said Roy, ‘and that just brushes the surface.’

‘Total recall? I don’t believe it,’ said Anne.

‘Yes. Every last detail. Every fact learned. Anything ever seen or ever done,’ said Roy.

I could easily test this. I thought of a date when I knew Roy and I were together a few years previously. ‘What were you doing on twentieth March 2027?’

'It was a pleasant Saturday, Mark. Which part of the day are you interested in?'

'When we were together.'

'We were together in the park and coffee shop between ten and twelve in the morning, and again when we flew over the Florida coast that afternoon and had the problem with the Cessna. I suspect that is your only memory of that day?'

Park? Coffee? That meant nothing to me, but the Florida flight was supremely memorable as we'd almost had to ditch the aircraft. I didn't remember the park or coffee. 'The park,' I said.

'You joined me while I walked Henry Matheson's dog,' said Roy. 'He was in hospital. We crossed the road and entered the park. The leaves were just starting to bud. You were wearing jeans, a lumberjack shirt, a quilted black North Face jacket and a Pepsi baseball cap. You trod in a puddle and your foot was soaked. In the coffee shop you ordered a muffin which you complained was dry and got it replaced with a Danish pastry. You wouldn't let me pay.'

'Okay, okay. I hadn't remembered any of that, but the wet foot brought it all vaguely back. You remembered what I was wearing? Even I don't remember what I was wearing, but it sounds about right.'

'Of course it is right,' he said confidently. 'My entity lets me actually see the event in my mind, but there's much more. I could describe which windows were open in the surrounding buildings. I can see all the cars parked in the streets adjacent to the park. Everybody we saw I could describe in detail. In fact,' he chuckled and continued, 'I might be able to jog your memory over the two girls. Wonderful legs. One had blonde hair almost down to her ass, just your type, short denim skirt and blue tights. The other had a lilac bobble hat, a duffle coat and leggings with cowboy boots. Remember?'

I tried to recall the girls. 'Yes, I vaguely remember the blonde, now you mention it.'

'Well, you would, wouldn't you?' He laughed. 'You've always drooled over blondes. Now do you believe me?'

Memories of Henry's dog and one of the girls were there, but in no detail. 'How far back can you remember?' I asked.

'Let me see, give me a moment,' Roy said and closed his eyes to think. 'Good God! I remember a warm and comfortable enclosure and, damn it all, the process of being born!'

'No!' said Anna.

'*Yes*, and I'm not sure I'd like to retain that memory. And, my first steps, being fed, bathed, dressed.'

'So why don't our own hippocampi enhance our memories and faculties?' I asked.

'We've talked about that in the rille. Our entities think that as their ancestors became part of their hosts, they lost some of their abilities. They became complacent in the minds of what was, remember, Stone Age humankind.

They lost their ability to improve their hosts. From Stone Age to present day, humankind made its own way forward. The hippocampi had provided the stimulus to "think", but it was only a fraction of the spark we receive from our new friends now. Maybe we'll need a reinvigoration process ourselves, but not for a few hundred thousand years.'

'Free up Crystal,' said Anna.

'I'm here,' said Crystal, and I noticed her eyes had cleared.

'Did you have the same sort of memories?' asked Anna.

'Not sure I want vivid memories of being born, but, yes, I can zero in on any day of my life and see all the details, not just of me, but all of the people around me. Christmas dinner with my parents. First discovering my sexual orientation when I met Jenny during astronaut training and that explained so many of my anxieties as a teenager,' Crystal said.

'Okay. We accept the memory thing. What else is different?' I asked.

Roy went on to talk about how it enabled him to link information together to improve his work, how his thoughts were extremely clear, and it was easier to concentrate.

'Why do you allow the thing to ever become the dominant person, then?' asked Bill.

'It depends what we're doing. It is not a permission thing, it is more natural than that,' said Crystal.

'We both see and do everything,' added Roy. 'There is no conscious decision who is in charge. We both are.'

'So why the strange look in the eyes?'

'It bothers you, not us,' said Roy. 'When you first amalgamate, it is necessary for the entity to take charge as the human component is in shock.'

'Why didn't you tell us all of this before Linda and I escaped?'

'We didn't know. They took us over, totally. We didn't understand what was happening to us then. They controlled our minds tightly to prevent us communicating. My entity was too worried to release me, even for a moment. We were in a constant battle with each other and I was kept suppressed. It was awful. I can, of course, remember every detail of it, including hitting Linda and trying to incapacitate you. All against my will, which is probably why we failed that morning when you emerged from your cabin. The entity had to learn how to fight and I was resisting handing over the information. They thought it would be easier to just have total control and even I didn't completely understand what was happening until several days later, Mark. Our entities had to start from the position of control. Ask this woman,' he said, indicating Vicky.

I looked and could see her eyes were clear. 'Well, Vicky, how do you feel about your LRP?'

She spoke hesitantly, 'I was very afraid when I realised that I'd been infected and did everything I could to resist. Eventually, it explained and I understood.'

'The entities now know to be gentle,' said Roy. 'They realise that once control has been achieved, it should be quickly released to allow them to work with us instead of against us. Mark, if my entity and I had worked together, there is no way you would have been able to beat me off that day outside your cabin. If they'd known as much about us then as they know now, they would not have taken me over in the way they did. Our resistance caused them to clamp down even more effectively on our free will.'

'Let me hear you explain it, Vicky?' Anna asked.

'I felt a sharp pain as it entered me then a swelling sensation as it moved from my hand, through my arm and up to my head. I fell to the floor, unconscious.'

Anna continued, 'What happened when you awoke?'

'I was standing and tried to look around, but it wouldn't let me. Gradually it eased its control and I could examine my surroundings. I was feeding the chickens. We, that is me and her, were seeing my past. A perfect vision of me came up from when, as a child, I was plucking a chicken with my grandmother. Every moment was real to me, even her chatting and sort of half singing, half humming a Beatles song, *Norwegian Wood* – I'm seeing and hearing it again now. It's wonderful,' said Vicky.

'Plucking chickens!' said Bill.

'Well, the LRP was trying to find out what I knew about them. Austro was feeding in front of us – she's always first to the food.'

'Austro?' Anna asked.

'It's an Australorp, a chicken breed. I didn't know that. Oh, wait a minute… yes… I see… Actually, I *did* know that. I'd seen it in a book as a child. My entity found it there, in that memory of me, as an eight-year-old, looking at the book – oh, yes, it was called *Raising Chickens* – it showed rare chicken breeds. She didn't know what a chicken was. It was just a strange alien creature to her,' said Vicky. 'The memory recall alone is wonderful.'

'Would you like to change back, Vicky?' asked Bill.

'No. I don't think so,' she said.

'What about—' I said, but Vicky jumped back into the conversation.

'No. I definitely *would not* like to change back. Thought I'd better clarify that,' she said.

'What about free will?' I asked.

Roy replied, 'It's a little strange, realising that you're no longer alone, but I now live happily with my entity. The benefits so outweigh any privacy issues which quickly fade into the background.'

'It's a bit odd at the moment,' said Vicky, 'but I'm getting used to it.'

I pointed over towards the Marine guards. 'Roy. Do you see that plinth-like object?'

'Yes,' said Roy.

'If we press the button on the top of it, your entities will instantly die, and we now have a simple medical procedure to remove them from you. Say the word and we'll do it,' I said.

Roy's eyes reverted to the strange infected stare. 'No. Don't do that! We trusted you.'

'Release Roy,' I said.

His eyes cleared, 'Mark, please don't do this. The symbiosis with the entities is wonderful. I would hate to lose the connection. It would be like a bereavement. Believe me. My entity is extremely anxious and frightened that we shouldn't have trusted you. I'm doing my best to calm him. You're talking about killing a living, intelligent being. Please reassure us that you will not kill them, Mark. We trusted you. *I* trusted you. I expect you to live up to your promise.'

'No. Don't panic,' I said. 'I only wanted to ensure you knew that we could free you quite easily if that was what you wanted.'

'Well,' said Roy, his eyes bright and clear, 'understand this, Mark. We *most certainly do* ***not*** need saving!'

'Okay,' I said and stood up. 'We're leaving here to discuss this further. Would you like some refreshments while we're gone?'

'That would be good,' said Roy. 'Linda's brownies?' He laughed.

‘She’s not on the moon this time, but we’ll find something,’ I said and left the geo dome with Anna and Bill.

17 Deliberations

This was becoming increasingly confusing. We'd come to the moon to wipe out a dangerous parasite, but the parasite was telling us that it was actually a valuable symbiote. The infected individuals were claiming that they were living harmoniously in their symbiotic relationship. How the devil was I to put this over to NASA?

Back in the com dome I needed a confidential session with Neil at mission control, but with Anna and Bill present to ensure that I didn't omit anything that was crucial.

Penny had been monitoring the communications desk while Dave and Pete were continuing to repair other consoles which had been damaged during the LRPs' control of Moonbase. We still couldn't send live video to Earth from anywhere except the com dome. It was very frustrating in this situation. I had to ask Dave and Pete to stop their repairs while I spoke to NASA..

'Hi, Mark. Neil here, over,' he said.

'Anna, Bill and I have just finished a session with Roy and Crystal, and I wanted to speak to you about it. There's a video on the way. Who else is with you there? Over,' I said.

After the interminable four seconds, 'Okay, Mark. I have Bob with me, and a couple of technicians are assisting. Over.'

‘Right, Neil, I think I’d prefer to keep this tight. Would the technicians mind leaving you to it for a while?’ I asked and added, ‘Over,’ as an afterthought.

‘Give us a moment, Mark.’

It was probably less than a minute before Neil continued, ‘Okay, Mark just Bob and me. Over.’

‘Who is Bob?’ whispered Bill.

‘Head of NASA. Dr Michaels,’ Anna replied quietly.

‘Oh, yes,’ said Bill.

‘I can see a serious problem arising. Over,’ I said.

‘Okay. Speak freely. We’ll listen. What sort of problem? Over,’ said Neil.

‘It’s complex,’ I said and tried to marshal my thoughts. ‘We’ve been talking at length with Roy Williams, Crystal Mitumba and Vicky Jones. They are all infected. Roy and Crystal, as you know, since before Linda and I escaped, and Vicky is a recent case.

‘As you are aware, Roy required safe passage before they would come to Moonbase for a conference in the geo dome. We brought the multidirectional projector into the room and had five Marines standing guard, including Mike Robertson. We were fully prepared if they became aggressive.

‘All three of them seem to be sharing their knowledge with their LRPs, including the newly infected Vicky. They all claim that the LRP gives them fabulous benefits including total recall of all memories and experiences, going back, would you believe, beyond birth to the time in the womb. They also claim improved mental skills and control over their bodies. Roy says his LRP slows his heart when sleeping. The memory claim is real. It was demonstrated comprehensively to me. An event years ago was described to me in the most extraordinary detail. You'll see it in the video which is on the way to you.

'I offered to free them of their parasites there and then, but none of them wanted that. It horrified them, in fact, as you'll see in the video. They say that they now live in harmony with their LRPs and don't want to change back. Over.'

'Do you think it is genuine?' asked Bob.

'Over,' added Neil quickly.

'Yes. It is certainly genuine as far as we can make out. Either that or it's a phenomenally cunning ruse. Over,' I said.

'How much memory can the LRPs hold? Over,' asked Neil.

'We don't think they hold the memories which are recalled, they just access them within the host's mind. Over,' I said.

'What do Anna and Bill think? Over,' asked Bob.

'I think it is a real symbiosis,' said Anna.

'There's a natural suspicion,' said Bill. 'But it seems to be real, as far as I can make out.'

'If it was anyone other than Roy I was speaking with,' I said, 'I'd say I was still suspicious, but I've known Roy for years and I do believe him. Over.'

‘And this memory thing, how do we know that is real? Over,’ asked Neil.

‘You’ll see in the video. I am certain it is real, beyond a shadow of a doubt. Over,’ I said.

‘The video file has just downloaded, Mark,’ said Neil. ‘Bob and I would like to watch it. Can you keep them as guests while we do that? Over.’

‘Yes,’ I said. ‘We’ll do that and Anna, Bill and I will take a break and discuss strategy further. Over.’

‘Sounds good. Won’t be long. Out,’ said Neil.

‘Doug,’ I called over personal intercom. ‘Can you change the guard on our guests. Ask them to find out if they’d like any more food or drink. If they want the toilets, ensure the area is irradiated afterwards.’

‘Will do, Mark.’

Anna, Bill and I made our way through to the common room, giving back the com dome to Penny and her team.

∞∞∞∞∞∞∞∞∞∞∞

The three of us tucked into a substantial lunch with eggs from the hens, beans and sausages.

‘It really bothers me,’ I said. ‘Roy wouldn’t lie to me and he is adamant he wants to keep the LRP.’

‘Yes, but they’re still dangerous,’ said Bill. ‘How do we *know* they won’t try again to take us all over?’

Anna said, ‘If they lulled us into a false sense of security, they could then make their move on all of us.’

'And how could we ever allow one of them back to Earth. It could be a disaster,' said Bill.

'It would be a ticking timebomb for ever,' said Anna.

'Yes. It's the fact that they can still totally dominate whenever they wish that worries me most,' I said.

'Yes, suddenly no longer Mr Nice Guy and everyone on Earth is assimilated… like the Borg in *Star Trek*!' Bill said and chuckled. 'Except it's a real threat.'

We'd just finished lunch when Penny called us through to the com dome to talk to NASA again.

'We've been thinking about this long and hard, Mark,' said Neil, 'and we feel we need to find out whether the attachment is genuine. This is the plan we suggest…'

We all listened intently.

18 The Test

Back in the geo dome after our lengthy call to NASA, we explained the test we wanted to conduct. All three of the infected exchanged glances. 'Are you sure you're comfortable with this, Crystal?' asked Roy.

'If it satisfies NASA, then I'm happy to do it,' she said.

'Okay, come with us,' I said.

Crystal rose from her seat and she, Anna and I left the geo dome with Bill following us armed with a projector. We took the minor walkway from the geo dome through to the main concourse, turned left and entered the surgery. We'd warned Krishna that we were coming, and he'd sent all the other medics but one away for a while. Gillian was no longer in any danger and was now recovering in ward one.

'My name is Krishna, Crystal. Diana is one of our nurses. Can I ask you to sit on the medical couch, please?'

Crystal sat still and Anna brought over the sample flask.

'Where would you like me to put the flask, Crystal?' she asked.

I noticed that Crystal's eyes had taken on the strange, infected look, which meant this was the LRP speaking.

'Rest it on my left shoulder with the entrance close to my neck,' said Crystal.

'No funny business. Straight into the flask,' I said.

‘We are an intelligence similar to your own. When we agree to something, we will follow it through… unlike, I might add, many humans,’ said Crystal.

‘Okay, but we’re watching carefully,’ I said, actually feeling that I had just demeaned myself.

The flask was duly positioned.

‘Okay, Crystal,’ said Anna.

We watched as one of the LRPs, crystal clear, emerged from the front of Crystal’s neck and made its way into the flask. Anna slotted in the cover plate, screwed down the lid and silicone sealed it.

Crystal rubbed her neck and said, ‘Hurts!’

‘Okay, Diana. Label the flask and place it in the sample cupboard. Lock it and bring me the key,’ said Krishna.

‘Set up one of those mini movement detectors inside the cupboard in case it decides to get out,’ I said.

‘How can it get out?’ asked Krishna.

‘We know they can. It happened with the one which infected me during my return to Earth. The silicone might stop it, but we’ve no way of being certain. The detector will at least alert us.’

‘Incredible,’ said Krishna.

‘This is just you now, Crystal?’ I asked, noticing the stare was gone.

‘Yes. God, it feels weird,’ said Crystal.

‘How?’ asked Krishna.

‘I feel empty, hollow. I don’t like it.’

Diana gave Crystal a hospital gown and asked her to change behind a screen.

With her being in a pressure suit, this took about twenty minutes. She emerged and entered ward two where the scanner stood, a large doughnut shaped machine with an attached medical gurney.

Crystal lay down on the gurney and there were a couple of short passes in and out of the doughnut. Diana then applied a drip device to deliver a radioactive fluid into her blood vessels. It highlighted them and helped the interpreter to see organs and other structures. We squeezed behind the radiation screen and watched the main scan.

‘Okay, Diana. Crystal can get dressed and get her to drink plenty of water. Mark, it will take me some time to analyse the scans,’ said Krishna.

‘We’ll wait and watch,’ I said.

Krishna sat behind a wall of technology with four monitor screens and as many controls as an Orion cockpit. I could see various cross-sections of Crystal. Analysis of the LRP’s shape and reflectivity in Krishna’s other patients allowed him to set up an alarm if the scanner spotted a similar object, even if it had changed shape. The only alarm was when we got to Crystal’s head and her two hippocampi came into view.

‘No sign of any abnormality or second LRP,’ he said confidently, twenty minutes later. ‘Can’t see anything unusual. She is a very fit and healthy woman.’

‘What if it has shrunk itself and wrapped itself around some organ or another?’ I asked.

‘Its chemical signature would still have set off the alarm,’ said Krishna.

‘Okay,’ I said, ‘Bill, irradiate Crystal, please.’

We returned to the main surgery and Bill played the projector over Crystal’s torso. It had no effect, so we were as sure as we could be that she was free of parasites.

‘Sit down again, Crystal, please,’ I said.

She sat on the medical couch. ‘I feel awful, Mark. Sort of dreadfully alone, abandoned.’

‘It could be just withdrawal symptoms,’ Anna said.

‘No, it is more emotional than that, as if I’ve lost a close friend or family member. Harrowing. An unpleasant sensation of real loss.’

‘Crystal,’ I said seriously, ‘we’ve done this to you to discover whether hosting the LRP really is something you want to continue to do. Are you sure this isn’t just a reaction you’ll get used to, like, as you say, a bereavement?’

She sat quietly, thinking about my question.

‘Yes, I could live like this, but I would much rather have her back. I was trying to remember when I first met Jenny. I could, but it was like seeing it on a monochrome

TV through thick fog. Almost as if the memory is as nothing, yet, with the entity inside me, I can recall that memory in realistic 3D Technicolor any time I wish and even experience the thrill of falling in love as if it's brand new.' She paused, 'Also, my memory of my first Orion launch is pathetic compared with the images, sounds and colours I experienced with the entity. I feel a great loss. Please return her.'

'You're absolutely sure?' Anna asked.

'Yes. Absolutely. I don't think I can live like this. You've cut half of my mind out of me and fogged my memories,' she said and began to weep. 'It worsens… as… each minute… passes.' Anna put an arm around her.

'Sorry, Crystal,' I said, 'but we need to keep you separated from your LRP for two days so that we can be certain it is not some sort of withdrawal symptom. That's the test NASA required.'

'No. Please, no,' she pleaded. 'I've changed my mind. I don't want to do this.'

'You and Roy agreed,' I said.

'I know, but I didn't think it would be so bad. Please, Mark. Please let me have her back. I imagine this is what having Alzheimer's would be like. Knowing something is missing It's awful.'

'Why do you call it "her"?' I asked.

'Because she's part of me, I suppose. She *knows* me. She *is* part of me. We *are* me now. I'm female so she is female. I think we choose their gender when they enter us. I don't think they consciously change sex to match ours. It is more natural than that. She's a she and you have cut her out of me.'

'We've made up a bunk for you in the scanner room,' I said, 'but you're free to use the common room for refreshments et cetera. We'd rather you didn't go anywhere else. Your LRP is secure. Roy will be staying in the geo dome. We'll ensure they are safe but guarded.'

On hearing that, she looked up at me and asked, 'Are you sure I'm safe, Mark? I felt real hostility from some of the Marines. You will protect us, won't you?'

'I promise, Crystal,' I said.

∞∞∞∞∞∞∞∞∞∞∞

'Computer, are there any areas without people at the moment?' I asked.

'Yes, the EVA dome is empty, plus the three buggies, Mark.'

Anna, Bill and I left the surgery and crossed to the EVA dome. I hit the safety cut-out, which prevented anyone from starting the air cycling process, and closed the door.

'Why the cloak and dagger?' asked Bill.

'I'm worried about the situation and concerned about my cabin being bugged,' I said.

'They aren't,' said Bill. 'I personally checked each of the cabins when they were opened. They're clean.'

'How do you mean about being worried?' asked Anna.

'Well, if we find that the LRPs are not harmful and are, in fact, beneficial, what will Earth say?'

'Yes, I see,' said Anna. 'They could never allow someone with an LRP to return to Earth.'

'They can't anyway,' said Bill. 'The Van Allen belts would kill them before re-entry.'

'No, Bill,' I said. 'We can choose a polar trajectory for re-entry which avoids the Van Allen belts completely. That, by the way, is classified. Only a handful of us are aware of it.'

'But no one can live on the moon indefinitely. Their bones and muscles would deteriorate if it were years,' said Anna.

'That is exactly what I'm worried about. Let's keep this conversation between us for the moment, but I'll be listening *very* carefully to every word that comes from Earth about this. I want you two to do the same.'

'What's next then?' asked Anna.

'Firstly, I have to brief NASA. Be there with me as I am going to be honest with them about the situation and want to discover how they react. Threatened or interested. Will they want to find out more or show a less curious standpoint.'

We returned to the com dome, respectfully evicted the crew who were in there and called Neil.

'Hi, Mark,' said Neil. 'How did it go? Over.'

‘Who is at your end? Over.’ I asked.

‘Just me. Fire away. Over.’

I spent the next ten minutes outlining the effect upon Crystal of having her LRP removed, then asked Bill and Anna to add anything they thought was relevant.

‘So, what now, Neil? Over.’

‘We obviously need more information, Mark. Your plan to talk to Crystal again over the next two days should fill in a lot of gaps. You have Roy and Vicky under guard? Over.’

‘Absolutely. Over,’ I said.

‘Then let’s see how the situation develops over the next couple of days. Over.’

‘Okay, Neil, will do. Out,’ I said and cut the connection.

‘He wasn’t alone,’ said Anna.

‘What? How do you know?’ asked Bill.

‘He was in the middle of a sentence, didn’t hesitate, but I definitely heard a cough in the background.’

‘You’re sure?’ I asked.

‘Positive.’

‘Come on,’ I said. ‘We have to go back to the geo dome to let our other two guests know what is happening.’

∞∞∞∞∞∞∞∞∞∞

'At last!' exclaimed Roy as we entered the geo dome. 'What happened with Crystal?'

'Interesting. We're leaving her without her LRP for the full two days, as agreed, so that we can understand how she feels about it,' I said.

'I should get back to the rille. I can't sit around here for all that time,' said Roy.

'What exactly are you doing at the rille?' asked Bill.

'We've created a habitat in part of the cave system and are reasonably comfortable. We've also made a discovery which we are trying to understand. Remember, combined with our entities, our intellectual abilities are seriously enhanced.'

'What sort of discovery?' I asked.

'I won't let you know until I am reassured that you will not harm any of us. Your random killing of us must stop,' said Roy.

'But you were trying to attack us and also trying to take over the world. You're *not* harmless!' I said.

'We haven't harmed any of you,' he protested.

'Blake is dead!' I said.

'With respect, Mark, it was you who smashed his faceplate!' Roy proclaimed.

'Because, at the time, the two of you were trying to stop Linda and I from escaping… and you damn near succeeded.'

‘Okay, I concede that, but all of that happened long before we discovered how wonderful the symbiosis with the entities is,’ he said in a more conciliatory fashion. ‘It has been a difficult learning curve for the entities too.’

‘That is exactly what we’re trying to ascertain, Roy. What have you discovered at the rille? Pure ice? Something else?’

‘I won’t discuss it until you return Crystal to us.’

‘Okay, but can you explain why you’ve taken the quantum particle and cosmic ray detectors from Moonbase? NASA is somewhat put out about it.’

‘Same answer. Return Crystal to us and also Vicky’s entity if you aren’t going to return it to her,’ said Roy.

‘Will you come back the day after tomorrow, then? About fourteen hundred hours.’

‘I will,’ he said.

‘Okay. Mike, can your squad escort Roy back to buggy one and see that he, and the LRP on his shoulder, leave the garage dome?’ I said.

‘No problem, Mark,’ said Mike and they left us in the geo dome with Vicky.

‘What about me?’ Vicky asked.

‘We’ll escort you back to the bio dome where you can continue to stay until this is resolved.’ Then I suddenly had an idea and said, ‘If you’d prefer to separate from your LRP, you can re-join the rest of us.’ I said.

‘There’s another flask over there,’ said Bill getting up and retrieving the empty container.

‘It won’t be harmed,’ I said.

This could be an interesting experiment. Would her LRP have gained so much control over her that she would want to remain with it in isolation, rather than join her friends and colleagues?

‘I don’t know how to make it exit,’ she said.

‘Give it back control,’ I said and watched for the change in the clarity and alertness in her eyes. ‘Right, LRP. The host wants you to leave her until we’ve resolved the situation. You have my word that you won’t be harmed. Bill, offer the flask to her neck.’

Vicky sat down again, and we watched as the LRP left from just in front of her ear and entered the flask.

‘Silicone seal it and mark it clearly as Vicky’s, Bill. Take it through to Krishna to keep safe. You okay, Vicky?’

She rubbed her neck. ‘That hurt. Yes, I’m okay. Feels weird,’ she said.

Once Bill had left to go to the surgery, I walked over and hit the multidirectional projector. There was no effect on Vicky so she must be clear.

‘What do you mean by “weird”?’ I asked.

‘Sort of vacant, an absence of something, but I don’t know what.’

We were just leaving the geo dome and she suddenly stopped. 'Oh, dear,' she said. 'All those memories are gone.'

'Explain.'

'Earlier, I was enjoying some lovely memories of playing in the park, when I was a child. Talking to school friends. Family holidays. The entity brought them to life, as if I was really there. I can't see them anymore.'

'Let's get you to the common room for a meal and coffee. You'll feel better after that,' I said.

'It's sad,' she said quietly.

'How sad?'

'I've lost something lovely, Mark.'

'Come on, let's talk about it over dinner,' I said.

Where on Earth, or rather, the moon, was all of this leading us?

19 Mob

Anna, Vicky and I could hear the mob before we entered the common room. I pushed open the door.

A group of ten or twelve crew were standing surrounding someone on the floor, jeering and shouting expletives. It was incoherent, but I was still able to hear short sections, as you do when in a crowd at a football game.

'We can't trust you!' – 'Fucking alien' – 'Go back to where you came from' – 'Evil lesbian scum' and so on.

'***Hey***!' I shouted at the top of my voice, '*What the hell's going on here*?'

The spectators moved back, and it became clear that Crystal was lying on the floor, in floods of tears, with Alexei Mirislov, the anaesthetist, and the nurse, Diana Mills trying to comfort her and crouching to protect her.

The crowd had dispersed by now, but I saw that all of them were military astronauts. Many of them continued to look at Vicky in a threatening manner too.

'Diana, Alexei, what's been happening?'

'We brought Crystal into the common room about twenty minutes ago to eat,' said Alexei. 'Several of this group of *animals*,' he looked around at the Marines, 'started baiting her with snide comments.'

'When our meals were ready,' said Diana, 'she was taking hers towards that table and Danny Mackay pushed her in the back and she went sprawling.'

'Shouldn't be walking around free. Damn alien-lover!' he said from where he was standing near the panoramic window and its wonderful view over moon's surface.

'Mackay, go and find Colonel Baker and bring him back here. *At once!*' I said.

Several of the others made as if to leave the common room.

'And the rest of you *stay* where you are. *No one* leaves this room, except Mackay… and I don't want another word from any of you.'

'She can't stop crying, Mark,' said Alexei.

'It could be withdrawal from the LRP's departure,' said Diana.

Crystal looked up at us and said, 'I don't want to live like this. Why do they hate me? I've done nothing wrong.' She returned to frantic sobbing.

'*Yes, you did*!' shouted British commando, John Dyson, in a heavy Cockney accent, 'You let the fucking things in to try to take us over. You and Williams. That ain't not doing nothing wrong!'

'*Dyson*! Didn't you hear me? Not another word.'

'But, sir! Those things hurt us and were controlling us. Inside our minds, for God's sake. It was awful!'

'Dyson, one more word and you will play no further part in this mission!' I said. He turned around and looked out over the moon's surface.

Alexei helped Crystal to her feet. Her tunic was covered in food from falling onto the plate.

'Did you get burned?' asked Diana, helping her to a table where she could sit.

'No. Hot and messy, but no burns,' said Crystal, grabbing some serviettes to wipe her eyes, then wipe the remains of her meal from her tunic.

Diana ran to the counter and returned with a damp cloth.

'I'm sorry this happened to you, Crystal. Doug will discipline the culprits and it will not happen again,' I said.

'I want my entity back,' Crystal said.

'So do I. I know how she feels,' said Vicky.

'Look,' I said. 'We must finish the experiment to discover whether what you are feeling is more than a withdrawal symptom. NASA will need to know, and it will be critical if you are ever to be allowed to return to Earth.'

At that moment, Doug walked into the common room and he was hit with a dozen of his men speaking at once. '*Quiet!*' he roared and came over to us. 'What happened, Mark?'

Alexei and Diana described the entire event again and Doug marched over to the Marines. 'I want you lot in the rec dome now! Wait for me there. I'm ashamed of the lot of you!'

‘Diana,’ I said, while Doug was letting rip into his Marines. ‘Take Crystal and get her cleaned up with a new tunic. We’ll wait here for you to return.’

‘I wasn’t involved,’ said Mikhail.

‘So why didn’t you stop it?’ asked Doug. ‘You’re a sergeant. I expect you to be more responsible than that. Go to the rec dome.’

The Russian started to speak but Doug said, ‘*Don’t answer*. Go to the rec dome! Computer, tell Mike to meet me in the rec dome.’

‘Contacting Mike, Doug,’ said the computer.

In short time the room emptied and there was just Alexei, Vicky and me remaining. Diana and Crystal returned a few minutes later.

‘What can I get you to eat?’ asked Diana.

‘I’d prepared a mushroom omelette. That would do fine. Thanks, Diana,’ said Crystal, still with the most unhappy of demeanours.

‘What do you make of this, Alexei? It was like a baying mob when we came in,’ I said.

‘Yes,’ he said. ‘Was not good. If you hadn’t come in when you did, it might have turned violent. I’ve never seen anything like it outside of a rival sports supporters brawl… and for well-educated and disciplined Marines to behave like that was quite extraordinary. They’re meant to be the cream of the crop.’

‘Well, it seems as if it was violent anyway. Someone pushed her to the ground,’ I said.

'She was pushed. It might not have been the intention to knock her over, Mark.'

'Nevertheless.'

Bill joined us and we all ate together to show sympathy to the two women. Neither of them wanted to speak much, but we managed to extract more about their feelings since the loss of their LRPs.

We'd finished eating when Doug poked his head around the door and indicated that we should follow him.

Bill, Anna and I made our way to the now empty rec dome.

'What on Earth came over them?' I asked.

'I think that word "Earth" has a lot to do with it,' he said.

'Explain.'

'These are elite Marines, whichever nation provided them. Their lives are normally all action. They envisaged an enemy occupying Moonbase, which they'd trained to storm and to recover the buildings. Continually in fear of and risking their lives. Get the job done and back home.'

'I see that,' I said.

'But the mission changed. Because of that change, most of them were taken over by the LRPs who exerted maximum control. They feel violated and some, when resisting control, were actually hurt. They were forced to do things they'd never normally have done, like attacking you and me. We saved them from that, but their minds had been invaded by the very enemy they were supposed to be fighting. It had a serious effect upon their attitude to the alien bugs.'

'Yes, but we knew we might need to adapt to circumstances.'

'Not the circumstances we're in now,' he said.

'How do you mean?'

'Suddenly,' Doug continued, 'they are bored senseless with nothing to do, knowing the enemy is at another location eight miles away and they aren't being allowed to do their jobs – to go the rille and blow the enemy out of the water. Even worse, they observe that management – you three – have invited two of the enemy, the very two who had brought the LRPs which attacked them to Moonbase, into their domain. They're extremely frustrated.'

'Bored? On the moon! Don't give me that, Doug. I don't care how frustrated they are, they need to follow orders and remain calm,' I said. 'Crystal's in a hell of a state after being separated from her LRP and we need to learn from her reactions to find out if what they say about the LRPs is true. We can't allow her to be intimidated.'

'No. I know,' said Doug. 'I should've spotted this as a potential problem, but I didn't. I know now and it won't happen again. I'm sorry, Mark.'

'You'll need to report it to NASA,' I said.

'I'll do that now, Mark.'

'Right,' I said, and Doug got up and left the rec dome.

Now Bill, Anna and I were alone.

‘This worries me even more,’ I said.

‘Yes,’ said Anna. ‘The way things are heading, it’s possible we could be taking Roy and his people back to Earth. That might have all sorts of implications, both among this group of Marines and, I hate to say it, at NASA too. What if they’re ordered, over your head, to attack and dispose of the LRPs?’

‘They wouldn’t,’ said Bill.

‘Don’t be so sure,’ said Anna.

‘You really think so? That’d be pretty drastic,’ I said.

‘Barbaric,’ said Bill.

‘They can’t stay forever on the moon,’ said Anna. ‘That means it becomes a situation where they could be endangering the Earth. Do you think our governments would tolerate that?’

‘No,’ I mused. ‘We need to keep an ear open. Bill, can you run through communication recordings since my last call to Neil when Anna reckoned she heard someone in the background. In fact, get over to the com dome now and listen to Doug’s conversation with NASA.’

‘Will do, Mark.’

‘But let’s keep our anxieties to ourselves,’ I cautioned.

20 Distrust

'I was asked to leave the com dome,' said Bill.

'They asked you to leave?' asked Anna.

'Mike said it was classified because it was military.'

'We could be getting side lined,' I said.

'We are. I listened to the recordings. They were pretty explicit. I was surprised they hadn't erased them.'

'You're sure you didn't misinterpret them?' I asked.

'Absolutely. Here's a copy,' said Bill, handing over a memory card. 'General Gilby definitely said not to tell you about their conversation and Neil confirmed it. And they've asked Doug to prepare a plan to take the Asimov Rille. Just a contingency plan they said.'

'But why did they ask you to leave the com dome during their communication?' asked Anna.

Bill shrugged. 'It's very distrustful.'

'I suppose they have to be prepared in case they do turn out to be violent,' I said.

'Yes, but why not talk to us about it?' said Anna. 'You're overall commander and I'm your deputy. Bill is your military adviser. Why keep us in the dark? It doesn't make sense.'

'Unless they're using us. Maybe assuming we'll lull the infected into a false sense of security until a trap can be sprung,' I said.

'What other weapons have they brought, other than the projectors?' asked Anna.

'There was a large container which Vlad and Ludvic transferred from Uspekh 2 to Dragonstar 4,' said Bill. 'I checked it out and it contains conventional weapons. I saw a heavy duty rocket launcher and a quantity of automatic rifles.'

'They didn't try to conceal those, though,' I said.

'Were you aware of them?' asked Anna.

'Yes,' I said, 'but only to be used as a last resort. Now it's starting to look as if it is part of a larger plan.'

We all looked down into our coffee. Why were the military trying to isolate us?

Anna asked, 'Do you think they have a plan to attack the infected, radiate them and let that be an end to the matter?'

'Let's keep collating and be careful with whom we share information,' I said. 'But it does worry me. It's certainly the way governments behave, but I'm surprised Neil would be a party to it.'

'He might not have a choice,' said Anna.

∞∞∞∞∞∞∞∞∞∞∞

Later in the day, I wandered into the common room for coffee and a snack. I noticed Doug ahead of me preparing his meal. I microwaved a packet of flavoured rice to go with some rehydrated salmon and then waited until I could see his meal was ready.

'Ah, Doug. We must catch up. Join me at the table over there,' I said, indicating one which only had two seats.

‘Be there in a minute,’ he said, and I made a beeline for it, sat, and hit record on my minicomp.

‘So, Doug, how’s the Dragonstar repair going?’

‘Very well. They’ve repaired one leg and are manufacturing a replacement for the mangled second.’

‘No other damage?’

‘No, Mark. It came off not too badly. I’ve posted two guards at the landing site. A bit worrying that they’ve stolen equipment from outside Moonbase.’

‘What, you mean the missing spectrometers et cetera? That is a bit strange. Any idea what they might be doing?’

‘No. That’s more your field, Mark. Must say that with lunar nightfall coming in a few days, protecting our assets will become much more difficult. They could even steal a lander and take an Orion back to Earth.’

‘Are those weapons from Dragonstar 4 safe, Doug? Where have you stored them?’

‘They’re fine. We put them in the garage dome and have two guards in there whenever the outer door is opened.’

‘So, how do you think we should proceed with the infected and the rille, Doug?’

‘I’ve been giving that a lot of thought. It’s a shame we can’t irradiate the inside of the rille. That would finish it there and then.’

‘But we might not want to. There seems to be a number of benefits to some sort of symbiosis with them, Doug.’

‘Well, that’s more your domain. I’ll just make sure you have military backup when it’s needed.’

‘You dealt with the mob?’

‘Yes, Mark. As I said, it won’t happen again.’

‘I hope not,’ I said.

‘I’ve suspended Dyson and Mackay.’

I doubted that would be enough and decided that I needed to take some steps to protect the infected.

∞∞∞∞∞∞∞∞∞∞∞

Bill, Anna and I met up in the rec dome last thing before the sleep period and we made some contingency plans. Bill had checked it for electronic bugs as well as LRPs.

In the morning, I found Vicky sitting alone at a table in the common room.

‘Hi, Vicky. How’re you feeling today?’

‘Okay. Able to live without the entity, but every now and again I remember the loss of the total recall she gave me.’

‘You’d still rather have the LRP?’

‘Absolutely, sir. It really is like losing a family member,’ she said.

I looked around the room and saw Anna coming in with Crystal. I watched the reaction of the Marines. A few looked at the black woman sullenly, but no one said anything, either derogatory or even a simple good morning. Jack Kane, one of the nurses, was seated near the kitchen counter and I saw him say hi to the two girls, but that was it.

'I'll see you later, Vicky,' I said and joined Anna and Crystal at the kitchen counter to make myself some breakfast; just a bowl of cereal and some toast. 'Join me when you've got what you want,' I said.

A few minutes later, the three of us were sitting at a table on the other side of the common room, away from the military contingent. The panoramic view of the moon's surface was spectacular. Shadows were growing as the fortnight long lunar day moved into its last third. The shadows exaggerated the smaller lunar features making the scene even more stark.

'How are you this morning, Crystal? It's been a day now,' I said.

'Awful, Mark. I don't want to live like this. It's as if I've lost half my mental abilities. My normal memory is as good as it ever was, but it isn't a patch on what I had with my entity,' she said, sitting back and looking the epitome of misery.

'What else? We need to know.'

'It's difficult to sleep. I kept waking up during the night. Before, I would close my eyes and she'd wake me up when we'd planned. She cut my need for sleep to two or three hours. Last night I slept nearly nine hours and I'm still not refreshed.'

'Is there any other effect?' asked Anna.

'My mind. I've lost some of my faculties. We've been working on quantum mechanics in the rille and I tried to think about the project last night. I hadn't a clue. I've lost the ability,' she said.

'How do you mean?' I asked. Could I get her to spill the beans over what was happening at the rille?

'I couldn't remember any of the equations or even the reasoning behind them. It's just a tangled fog.'

I guessed she hadn't realised that she was giving us an insight into their activities. 'What's the project?' I asked.

'We're linking quantum gravity with general relativity. It was all so clear, but now it's just mental chaos.'

'Would you like one of the Moonbase laptops?' I asked. *Good grief, this was fringe science!*

'Oh, no!' she exclaimed. 'That wouldn't help at all, we were working in five dimensions.'

I looked at Anna and saw that her eyes had widened at the same time as mine. Was Crystal serious? Were the infected really working on five dimensional quantum mechanics? Linking general relativity with quantum gravity had been the scientific puzzle which physicists on Earth had been trying to resolve for more than a hundred years.

'Tell us more,' I said.

Crystal pulled herself out of her slouch and sat upright. She looked annoyed and was staring at me. 'No,

I don't think so, Mark. I shouldn't be talking about it at all really. Tosh wants us to keep it to ourselves.'

She'd rumbled my questions. 'How is Tosh?'

'He's fine.'

'What's he working on these days?' I asked casually.

'Sorry, Mark. I spoke out of turn. I shouldn't say anymore, even if I could remember it.'

'But we're interested, Crystal. Trying to understand.'

'Then ask Roy or come to the rille. I'm not saying anything else until I get my entity back. Being without her is torture. I'm not thinking straight.'

'Roy will be back tomorrow, and we'll talk it through,' I said. I'd blown my chance of extracting any more information from Crystal.

21 Suspicion

The rest of that day saw our communications in the com dome brought back to their standard prior to being smashed, but NASA were still frustrated by the lack of access to the many particle detectors the infected had taken. Dragonstar 5's legs were replaced by late afternoon and the Canadarm, attached to buggy three, was used to lift the Dragonstar, one side at a time, to complete the repair. Several technicians worked long after the start of the normal rest period, to strip and rebuild the faulty thruster and clear the fuel system from the main engine which had failed.

The next day was Crystal and Vicky's second day without the LRPs and I'd set up for Roy to return for a further conference. I caught up with Doug prior to him arriving.

'Roy is on the way from the rille, Doug. He's bringing another infected person, Mary Carter, with him,' I said.

'Same procedure?' he asked.

'Yes. Ensure either you or Mike is there. I don't think I can trust the Marines on their own any longer. Remember that Roy might be carrying the LRP from the buggy. Allow them a safe distance before irradiating the buggy.'

'No problem.'

'Make sure there is no chance of any rogue Marine deciding to attack them. That Dyson guy… I'd rather he wasn't involved,' I said.

‘He’s not. He’s still suspended. We will take care. I’ll set four guards for the geo dome for your meeting too,’ said Doug.

‘No. We won’t need them. I’ll take the multidirectional projector with me and we’ll have it beside us if there is any aggressive move.’

‘I’d rather have armed personnel with you,’ said Doug.

‘Bill will be there, and he’ll be carrying a taser. We’ll be safe enough. The projector will be switched on, so it would only take a single strike to kill them all.’

‘Well, let it be known that I am not comfortable with your actions, Mark. No point in having us professionals here if you’re going to ignore our advice.’

‘I want to try to make it a relaxed environment and it’s difficult to achieve that with four armed observers,’ I said.

‘Yes, I see. Okay. I’ll head to the garage dome and Mike or I will bring them to you.’

‘Thanks, Doug.’ I said as he turned and left the common room. The situation was becoming very convoluted.

I walked through to the com dome and found Penny on duty. I sat beside her.

‘Need to ask a favour, Pen,’ I said.

‘No prob,’ she replied, colouring as she always did when we spoke. I supposed that it would always be impossible for either of us to forget our brief affair.

‘I need to trust you with absolute confidentiality,’ I said.

‘What crime are you asking me to commit?’

I laughed. ‘Not quite that bad. I just want you to ensure that no one is watching the live feed from the geo dome when we start our meeting with Roy.’

‘You want me to cut it if someone attempts to?’

‘No one should have any access to it without clearance from me. That’s what to tell them.’

She looked at me with a puzzled expression. ‘Okay. You can rely on me.’

‘Thanks, Pen.’

∞∞∞∞∞∞∞∞∞∞

I’d arranged a larger conference table and also had the crew bring in some snacks and a coffee flask. Bill, Anna and I sat on one side with the multidirectional projector between me and Bill. On the other side were Vicky and Crystal. The two LRP containers sat in front of Crystal and Vicky. The door opened and Mike entered with Roy and Mary. Mary was a physicist, working on space radiation, who had also been the deputy commander of Moonbase under Blake.

Mary put her hand on Crystal’s shoulder before sitting down. Once they were both seated, Mike asked, ‘You sure you don’t want me to stay?’

‘No, we’ll be fine, Mike, we have this,’ I said, touching the multidirectional projector.

When they left, I said, 'Thanks for returning. Mary, lovely to see you again.'

Slightly glazed brown eyes looked back at me coldly, but she said, 'Yes. You're well?'

'I am,' I said.

'How are you, Crystal?' asked Roy.

'Devastated. I feel hollow and abandoned. It's the most dreadful experience. I want my entity back. *Badly! Now*!' she said.

'Okay,' I said. 'Let's get started. We've been watching and listening to both Crystal and Vicky over the last two days to get a feel for their attachment to their LRPs. While Crystal seems at a total loss, Vicky is able to deal with the separation. That indicates that they're not essential to you and time heals.'

'*Not at all!*' said Vicky loudly, surprising me with her unexpected intervention. 'I'd like it back. It did me no harm and it improved my memory beyond belief. I'll never feel the same without it.'

Anna said, 'But when we spoke earlier today, you seemed reconciled to living without it.'

'Yes, but I'm military,' said Vicky. 'I understand that I was brought here to deal with these entities. I'm hardly going to be allowed to become one of the enemy, am I? That doesn't mean I don't want to. I'm going to miss her… dreadfully.'

'Mark, please give Crystal her entity,' said Roy.

I nodded. Bill cut the silicone and Crystal unscrewed the container. She reached in and I assumed it entered her hand. She jumped as if receiving a shock, her eyes glazed, and she sat back in the chair. Within a couple of seconds her eyes cleared, and the real Crystal smiled back at me.

'You will *never* understand how wonderful that was. Marvellous. Like being reunited with a sister or mother you'd been told was dead. Thank you,' Crystal said.

'Vicky, I can't let you become infected again,' I said.

'Well,' said Bill, 'what's going on at the rille?'

'The ultimate proof that humankind needs the entities,' said Roy.

'Explain,' I said.

'You know me, Mark. I'm a geology freak, not a physicist or mathematician. It's why I brought Mary,' he said.

'Yes,' I acknowledged.

'Well, in these few short weeks,' said Roy, 'we've cracked the unification of quantum gravity with general relativity,' said Roy. 'It all became clear, then a few experiments by Mary and Jenny with particle detectors followed by theory testing with the alpha magnetic spectrometer and, bingo, the universe is a different place. Trying to get one's head around space-time bending and the expanding universe becomes simple. With one of our entities, a child could do it. They enhance our minds a hundredfold.'

‘Can you explain some of this to us poor humans?’

‘Sorry, Mark,’ said Mary, ‘I don’t mean to be disparaging, but you wouldn’t understand. And Roy is exaggerating at a “hundredfold”, but the enhancement is substantial.’ Mary had always been more technical in her conversations.

‘Damn it all, you have to be able to explain it to NASA or your claims are meaningless. What can you give us to send to Earth?’

Mary said, ‘Top physicists and mathematicians will understand, though even they will struggle. That’s why the unification has not been solved in a hundred years since Niels Bohr first began to get the flavour of it. Even Einstein didn’t get it.’

‘We need something, Mary, or we’ll be left with only bad solutions for Moonbase and those of you in the rille. You’re still our deadly enemies. Don’t you understand that?’

‘Yes, we do understand,’ said Roy.

He reached into a pocket and removed a memory card. ‘This contains formulae for a method of warping space.’

‘As in “warp factor eight”?’ Bill asked sarcastically.

‘Well, no,’ said Roy. ‘That’s all nonsense, but this explains how distant places in space-time can be joined temporarily to allow movement between them.’

‘What, the folding of space idea?’ asked Anna.

Mary said, ‘Sort of, but there’s no point me trying to explain it to you. Send those files to the astrophysics departments at Amherst, Massachusetts or Cambridge in England, and they'll recognise that it is ground-breaking science. If we are destroyed, humanity will *never* forgive you when it realises what you did! It would be good if you didn't forget that.'

For Mary to speak in that tone certainly showed her conviction to what she was saying. 'Anna, take that through to the com dome and get Neil to send it to those universities. Tell them we need their urgent opinion,' I said. She dashed straight out of the geo dome with the card.

'What now?' asked Roy.

'Are you telling us that what you've discovered will open the entire universe to us, or what?' I asked.

'We think so,' said Roy.

Mary said, 'In fact, we're pretty confident. We can't prove it with the equipment available to us, but we've proven the principle and that data card contains the scientific proof.'

'What do you want from us?' I asked.

'To allow us to join you and add entities to each of you so that you can enjoy the same benefits,' said Roy.

'Phew! You *are* joking?' said Bill.

'I think that memory card will need to be pretty convincing if you want us to follow that path,' I said.

'Mark, I know you like a brother, but I don't know Bill or Vicky, can we talk alone,' said Roy.

'Bill and Anna are my two prime advisers. I trust them both implicitly,' I said. 'I can ask Vicky to leave the room.'

'Yes, do that,' said Roy.

'Sorry, Vicky. Can you wait outside the geo dome door?'

When she'd gone, I said, 'You can speak freely now.'

'Are we not being recorded?' Roy said, pointing at the camera.

'Yes, but the high bandwidth link to Earth is only working from the com dome. We're recording this. We can lose it if we think the conversation is too sensitive to send to NASA, and I have someone making sure no one watches us live.'

At that point, Anna returned to the geo dome and took her seat. 'The files are on the way to NASA with a note from me about forwarding them to the universities,' she said.

'You're absolutely sure these two are trustworthy?' Roy asked.

'Certain beyond the possibility of doubt. I'd trust them with my life,' I said.

'Okay,' said Roy, lowering his voice. 'We're not stupid, Mark. Even if we convince you, NASA might not be impressed and, let's face it, there will be generals and world leaders who must be being kept in the picture. They most certainly will *not* allow us to return home, even if we can offer a gateway to the treasures of the universe.'

'And?'

'I think that there will be an attempt to destroy us!' he said.

'You might be right,' I said. 'Do you have a solution?'

'We do think the best solution is to take over all of you. That would remove the immediate threat, but our failure last time has left us under strength. There are over twenty of you?'

'Twenty-eight including Vicky,' I said.

'We do not have that number of entities and will not have for a couple of days. We are dubious that we will be allowed that long,' said Roy.

'I'd agree with that analysis,' said Bill. 'I think the military will move sooner than that.'

'You said it was the best solution. Is it your only solution?' I asked.

'No. We could destroy you, but that would leave Earth in the same dilemma of what to do with us. I fear that a second mission to recapture Moonbase would then be likely to involve a nuclear solution – they'd wipe us out totally,' said Roy.

'Is there a third solution?'

'We retreat to the rille. You could come with us. We're fairly sure your current weaponry couldn't penetrate our underground habitat,' said Roy.

'They have rocket launchers and automatic weapons,' said Crystal. 'The Marines were talking about them.'

I didn't say anything but was shocked that there could have been such loose talk in the common room while Crystal was there. Maybe the military weren't as professional as they thought they were.

'It wouldn't solve anything, Roy,' I said. 'You'd be trapped, and Earth would send whatever armaments it thought would do the job to get you or us out.'

'Do you have any better ideas?' asked Crystal.

'No, but we certainly need to stop a recording of this meeting reaching Earth,' I said.

'I'll deal with that,' said Bill.

'Do you two understand what we could be getting into here?' I asked. 'Alien entities are asking us to trust them rather than our own people at NASA. We are potentially becoming traitors to the whole of mankind.'

'I believe Roy and I watched Crystal very carefully,' said Anna. 'We cannot allow them to be hurt and, frankly, I'm curious about joining them.'

'You'd like to play host?' asked Roy. 'You have Vicky's entity in that flask.'

'Are you sure it will leave me with control?' asked Anna.

'Let it join with you now. When it is inside you, I'll explain to it easier than you could,' said Roy.

Anna looked at me enquiringly.

'Bill?' I asked. 'No turning back if we take this step.'

'Yes. Try the experiment,' said Bill. 'I'd like to see if you can fool the others while hosting one. Mark and I can also keep an eye on you and see if we can spot other differences which could give you away.'

I used Bill's knife to cut the silicone and passed the flask to Anna.

Anna opened it slowly, removed the cover slide and peered inside. Looking over her shoulder, I saw the LRP making its way to the lip of the container.

'What do I do?' asked Anna.

'Offer up the back of your hand. She will know it is intentional then,' said Crystal.

I watched Anna turn her right hand towards the flask. Contact was made.

'*Ouch*!' Anna cried as we saw the LRP vanish through her skin and she collapsed back into the chair. I reached out to steady her.

'Anna has agreed to work with us. Release her,' said Roy.

Anna's face immediately relaxed, and I watched her eyes return to normal. 'What does it feel like?' I asked.

'Ooh! Weird. I feel like I'm high on something. There are pictures flashing through my mind, well… no, not pictures… sort of memories, but brought to life. Oh, my!'

'What?' I asked and Anna started crying.

'What is it?' asked Bill.

'Brian. Oh, it's Brian!'

'Who's Brian, Anna?' I asked looking at Bill who shrugged his shoulders.

'My brother,' she sobbed. 'He died four years ago, but I can see him as real as if he were here… oh, now more… my twenty-first party and he's fallen in the pool.' She laughed out loud.

'Anna. Take control. Can you control it?' I asked.

Roy said, 'Tell it to stop with the memories and quieten down.'

'How? How do I do that?' she asked.

'Just think it,' said Crystal.

Anna wiped her eyes and her face relaxed. 'Yes. I see. Yes. Oh, yes. Can I? Wow, I see. I do. I can.'

Bill and I looked on with suspicion. Who was she speaking to? The LRP? I saw her eyes change to the dazed look of the infected, but it was only for a couple of seconds, then they returned to normal.

'I am in control,' she said. 'It's truly amazing. I can't help calling up images of Brian and the two of us with our parents. It is… I can't express it strongly enough… amazing. No other words will do.'

'Ask it to leave you,' I said. 'Now!'

Anna looked at me in shock. 'What? Why?' she said. 'That's not a fair test.'

'Do it,' I said.

She put her hand to the flask and the LRP left her. 'Oh, that hurt. Oh dear, I'd like more time with her. I thought we were going to let me live with her for a while to see if we could fool the others.'

'You feel okay?' I asked.

'Yes, but I want more,' said Anna.

'In what way? Like you want more heroin or more chocolate?'

She laughed. 'Definitely more chocolate! Oh, the memories are still there, but not in the same detail.'

'Okay, Anna. Take it back.'

'Her. It's a her,' she said putting her hand to the flask entrance again. Her skin touched the thing and it vanished into her body.

'Oh, wow. That is so good, Mark.'

'Right. Now we need to think about the next step,' I said. 'Roy, we cannot come with you.'

'The military will attack us,' he said.

'How can we mitigate that?' I asked.

'I don't think it will happen immediately if we give you an invite to visit the rille. That would give us more time,' said Roy. He pulled a small container, about the size of a pack of playing cards, out of an inside pocket. 'There are four entities in here, Mark. See how Anna is getting on with hers tomorrow and if you feel safe, you and Bill could absorb one as well. Don't be observed in those first few minutes though.'

‘I’m not sure we’re ready for that, Roy,’ I said.

‘Then keep them somewhere safe until you are – I’m certain you will be eventually,’ said Roy. ‘The military will come for us ultimately. When they do, you hang back. If possible, stay in Moonbase.’

‘Why? You mustn’t kill them,’ I said.

‘No, we won’t hurt them, but if you have absorbed the entities, you will not want to be anywhere nearby as there’ll doubtless be a lot of irradiation,’ said Roy. ‘I should get back and you need to secure that video. I presume you’ll check that no one saw it live?’

‘Of course,’ said Bill.

‘Mark. A couple of other points. I am putting my trust in you now. Don’t let me down,’ said Roy.

‘Go on,’ I said.

‘Tosh is working on a method of strengthening our, or, rather, our entities’ resistance to the projectors. He is working flat out on it. One other point.’

‘Yes,’ I said.

Roy passed over a piece of paper. ‘This has coordinates upon it, moon coordinates. Get them to someone you trust on Earth. Three entities are buried at that location. It is sixteen kilometres from here so outside the likely range of any small nuclear explosion. Humankind must not be deprived of the advantages of the entities. Someone must know the location. Keep it safe.’

‘I will,’ I said. If Roy thought the stakes were this high, it needed to be treated seriously. ‘You really think they would nuke this site?’

‘Yes. We’re pretty certain that will be the outcome if they think we could make it back to Earth,’ said Roy.

I called for Mike on the intercom and he entered with Mikhail.

‘Roy, Mary and Crystal are returning to the rille. Please provide safe passage for them,’ I said.

‘And Vicky? She’s outside the door,’ said Mike.

‘No, she’s no longer infected and is now free to re-join her Marine squad,’ I said. ‘Send her in to us.’

Mike, Mikhail, and the visitors left the geo dome. Vicky returned to sit opposite us.

‘Vicky,’ I said, ‘you can return to your squad, but I wanted to suggest that you don’t talk about how much you liked your LRP. It could lower morale. Can you keep it to yourself?’

‘Yes, but please let me be considered if you need someone to test the symbiosis over a longer period,’ Vicky said.

‘You’d risk a second infection?’ Bill asked.

‘At the drop of a hat,’ she said. ‘But I won’t talk about it in the meantime.’

‘Thank you, Vicky. You’re free to go. Report to your commander,’ I said.

‘Will do,’ she said as she got up and left. Anna, Bill and I were alone again.

‘Do you think I’m safe walking around Moonbase?’ asked Anna.

‘Yes, why?’ I asked.

‘I wouldn’t want to get accidentally irradiated. It would hurt my entity. She’s anxious about it.’

‘Yes, I see. You’ve already built up that sort of rapport with it?’ I asked.

‘Yes. She’s very much part of me.’

‘There is already a rule about no casual use of the projectors. NASA is worried about the effects on the human body, so there shouldn’t be any danger of being within range of casual projector fire. You feel protective of her?’

‘Very much so. I already feel that she’s integral to me.’

‘You’d better ensure there are no lapses in control. Those big blue eyes of yours are pretty magnetic. Any dullness in them will certainly trigger suspicion and the Marines are already far too jumpy for my liking.’

‘I’m going to deal with that recording,’ said Bill. ‘I think it’s best that the memory card develops a fault too.’

‘Yes. And ensure the original is wiped beyond recovery,’ I said.

‘I’ll record data over it right now,’ he said.

Our little secret meeting ended.

How did I feel about this? I was loyal to NASA. All its objectives and principles were second nature to me. If I was considering being disloyal to NASA, it also meant that I was being a traitor to the United States of America and the whole of humanity. My dilemma was frightening.

It was now clear to me that the LRPs were not a threat to any of us or the world in general. They offered the chance of enhancing us, but even more importantly, they were an intelligent alien species and should be studied, not destroyed.

I didn't know how I was going to be able to square this with my own conscience or with NASA.

'Sorry, Neil,' I said. 'We'll try to find out how it got recorded over. I'd have liked you to have been able to watch it. Over.'

'You're convinced the LRPs are no longer a danger to us, Mark? Over,' he said.

'Yes, pretty well. Let me say ninety-eight per cent but it would be very difficult to get to one hundred per cent with my own experience in the Orion with Linda. That gave me a rather jaundiced view of them. I'll never forget that torture. Over.'

'I'll get back to you, Mark. Can I just point out that I have top brass military with me now, so the Moonstruck mission is no longer solely my responsibility? Over.'

'Okay, Neil. Understood. Over.'

'Make your judgement calls with care, won't you? Over.'

'Will do. Over,' I said. I believed Neil was giving me a veiled warning.

'Good luck. Out.'

I sat back in the chair.

'Not good,' said Bill.

'It seems he is not too happy either,' I said.

'No. He definitely wanted you to read between the lines,' said Anna.

'Is that you or the LRP judging that?'

‘A bit of each. I seem to have more empathy with her being present. Also, I no longer like the LRP designation. It is not a parasite.’

‘You’re still convinced the symbiosis is just that, and not a parasitic take over?’ asked Bill.

‘Absolutely certain, Bill. I am thinking more clearly and slept extremely well last night. So refreshed when I awoke. My entity told me that she’d slowed my heart rate, lowered my temperature and lengthened my respiration.’

‘Sounds good,’ I said. ‘What are we going to do then?’

‘I’d like to try the bug myself,’ said Bill.

‘Okay, but we’ll need to keep ourselves well away from any chance of getting hit by a stray projector blast. Let’s leave it until later today so that we can have the evening and overnight to adapt. I’ll radio Roy and set up for us to visit the rille for some time tomorrow,’ I said. ‘That will give us at least another day before the military will act.’

‘You’re going to try it yourself?’ asked Anna.

‘I have to. I can’t just rely on you two.’

‘You’ll need to keep Doug in the picture somehow or he’ll get suspicious,’ said Anna.

‘He can’t be told about our becoming hosts,’ I said.

‘No, of course not. You’ll need to invent a story,’ she said.

‘Yes, I’ll tell him that visiting the rille is a reconnaissance and investigatory mission. That should give him reason to wait if there are already orders in the pipeline. He’d want to make use of our information as intelligence before starting an attack.’

‘He might want to provide cover for us,’ said Bill.

‘I’ll think of a way of getting around that,’ I said.

∞∞∞∞∞∞∞∞∞∞

Later in the afternoon, I was in my cabin, as we called our personal quarters, with Bill and Anna. She sat on the chair while Bill and I used the bunk. We had a long hard talk with Anna about how the entity was changing her abilities. I too felt that “parasite” no longer applied to these creatures. The change in her went deeper than just her new abilities – I’d known Anna since I’d entered astronaut training, yet she was now making arguments which were certainly more carefully thought through and always positive. She hadn’t been so confident in the past. This indicated that the entity was affecting not only her mental abilities, but also her reasoning and understanding of situations.

‘My dexterity is better too,’ she said.

‘How do you mean?’ Bill asked.

‘Watch,’ she said and balanced a pen by its point on the tip of her finger.

‘We all know that’s easier on the moon,’ I said. ‘The lower gravity helps the pen resist leaning off centre quickly enough to fall and if you have good reactions, you can keep it upright.'

The pen sat, motionless on her fingertip. I couldn't see her making any adjustments.

'Okay. You do it, Mark,' she challenged and tossed the pen over to me.

I placed it point down on my finger then released it. I could balance it, yes, but after a few seconds, my adjustments became ever more erratic until gravity finally won the tussle and the pen fell to the floor.

Bill picked it up. He was better than me, but he still lost it within about fifteen seconds.

Anna took the pen back. 'Watch!' she said.

She dropped the pen, point first, from a height of maybe ten centimetres, onto her finger. In two seconds, it was under control and motionless. She moved her finger upwards, slid her hand to the right and it descended on her second fingertip – again it was stationary in a couple of seconds. Same again onto her third finger, then her pinkie. She tossed it higher and it came down onto the back of her hand, where, in no time at all, it sat as if superglued into position.

'Amazing,' I said.

'And memories, Mark,' said Anna. 'All my calculus from college is there at my beck and call. It's astonishing. I really can believe they are working with five dimensional physics, especially with Mary in their midst. She's a brilliant astrophysicist, you know.'

'Yes, you're probably right. Well, Bill, ready to take the plunge?' I asked and took out Roy's container.

'Yes, ready,' he said.

'No turning back for any of us if we take this step,' I said.

'It is the right thing to do,' said Bill.

The lid was on the large side of the box, so it opened very much like an old cigarette box. Within, four entities were moving around. It was interesting that there was no attempt to leap upon me or invade without permission. Was this the result of them growing within a symbiotic rather than a parasitic environment? Bill offered up the back of his hand and jerked as one of the entities jumped onto him and vanished within him; I steadied him with my other arm until he recovered. I looked at him. His eyes were clear. He nodded that he was okay.

I moved the box into my left hand and offered the back of my right. After the nightmare infection I'd had on the Orion on my return to Earth with Linda, what the hell was I doing? Surely this was a crazy action.

'Ouch!'

23 Two Become One

After the short, sharp pain of entry, as others had said, I felt the entity move rapidly up my arm, the side of my neck and enter my brain, although it presented more like an entry into my mind.

A warm flush moved through my entire being, spreading from my face, down through my body and into the farthest extremities. Even my toes seem to be glowing, but it quickly faded, and I guessed my entity was exploring its new host. How did I feel about that?

I turned and looked at Bill, then at Anna, firstly seeing them as aliens – whoa – they were strange and unfamiliar alien beings, then, all of a sudden, they were once more the friends and colleagues they actually were. I wondered if my eyes had glazed during that first encounter with what must be weird creatures for the entity. Did my eyes then clear as my own mind came to the fore, recognising people I knew well? Surely these entities already knew humans. Was it all part of a new adjustment within a different human?

'You okay, Bill?' I asked.

'Yes,' he said. 'You?'

'Yes,' I said then looked at Anna. 'And what's amusing you?'

She laughed. 'I know what you're both experiencing. Amazing, isn't it?'

We both agreed.

Short flashes of memory were appearing and fading within my mind. Some important, like meetings with Neil and other top NASA officials, and some insignificant, like the shock of a curry I'd once ordered which unexpectedly turned out to be a vindaloo, or opening a gift from my parents as a child one Christmas. It… no, not it… *he* was exploring me, understanding me, but I was, simultaneously learning about myself. I took a sharp breath as I experienced the last moments of my mother's fight against cancer as if it was happening anew. I didn't want the death memory but treasured that final smile she'd given me a few minutes before her last moments arrived. How lovely to see her face again.

I saw my exam results and the beaming grin of my chemistry teacher as I showed him the grades – and then the bleeding and broken nose from a deliberate punch in the scrum of a barbaric foreign school game called rugby.

Worse. A memory of the first entity flicked through my mind. The new entity realised what had happened, that I'd been overcome and controlled and that I'd tried to tell Linda to kill us both. He was shocked by the first entity's reactions. He recognised its mistake; then I seemed to be inside that first entity, feeling its anguish at the sickness which began to pervade its being, its knowledge that it was dying and the agony it inflicted upon me when it thought I was the cause of its demise. It existed no more. It was gone. He was sad for it, but deeply upset for the harm it had done to me. I had to choke back tears. He was more hurt by my pain than the member of his own species' death. He knew the way the entity had behaved was wrong but could also see why it had behaved that way. A dreadful mistake made through mutual ignorance, during those early days of encountering our species, and before realising the extent of the opportunities our two species offered each other for the future.

I was physically shaking. I'd experienced the torture again and been overcome by the pain it had showered me with. My new entity appreciated the hurt I'd suffered and offered a warmth to me, showing it knew what had happened and it would never occur again. He loved me. He wanted what was best for me.

'Mark! *Mark, **Mark***! Are you all right?' asked Anna, who was kneeling in front of me, holding my hands as my faculties returned.

'Yes. Don't worry,' I said. 'It found the memories of the first entity which was killed as we passed through the Van Allen belts. It felt some of my pain and anguish as well as seeing its death. He then comforted me through the exposure which was frightening for both of us. I'm okay now.'

'I'd like some time alone with mine,' said Bill.

'We should eat,' said Anna. 'It would be best if we ate together and then spent some time getting to know our new friends overnight, alone in our cabins. Less chance of giving ourselves away if we stick together when in public.'

‘Yes. Let’s do that,’ I said and cautioned my entity to not take control while we were in the same room as other humans. I warned Anna and Bill to do likewise.

∞∞∞∞∞∞∞∞∞∞∞

During the meal, we continued to speak in hushed tones about our experiences with the entities. Several times my entity flashed memories up, asking about why a particular day, time, location or event was important, learning about my life. In the end I had to tell him to stop as I was concerned about looking preoccupied – something I would never be if I was in company.

Back in the safety and privacy of my cabin, it was different. I got into my bunk, dimmed the lights, lay back and relaxed, granting him full control.

Wow! Suddenly, he was all over me, opening and closing scenes from the past. We spent time in an astrophysics lecture I’d attended, and it was all so easy to understand this time. I’d had such a struggle with some of the applied mathematics, but now it was simple, child’s play. He made me break the problems down into manageable chunks then solve each, one at a time. Why had vectors so bemused me? They were obvious now.

What’s this? I was spinning around in mid-air!

Someone was gripping my hands. *Don’t let go!*

What the devil? Oh. I was a young child on the beach, being swung round and around and around at arm’s length by my father. My laughing and screaming was real again and his sparkling eyes and pleasure at the expression on his son's face was wonderful to behold.

Another scene, and he'd made me sit in a shallow trench on the beach and constructed a sand racing car around me, with a rubber ring for a steering wheel and spade handle for a gear stick.

We were both laughing, and my lovely mum was taking photographs. Always taking them but never in them. I must find them when I get home. But, no, I needn't. Untaken pictures of her were all here, in my mind – every time I'd ever looked at her was stored somewhere I could never hope to find on my own, but he could find them for me. There they were. In full colour, lifted out of the obscurity of some forgotten mental recess. How delightful. Anything I had ever seen, even fleetingly, could be enjoyed again but in crystal clarity. It seemed impossible, but in fact was real.

A switch of scene. What a shock! I was kissing Brenda Wilkinson under an octagonal table. It was junior school. We were ten. I smiled at the innocence of the memory. My first kiss. I felt the warmth, the wetness and the back of my hand wiping it away. I wanted to laugh. But now it wasn't like that. I felt fear. He'd found another, much less innocent memory.

Anxiety filled every part of my being. I saw myself stealing a toy rocket from Duke's Emporium. It was red and blue. Its fins were long and tapered. The top had a steel tip and there was space to insert a percussion cap, so that if you threw it, when the point impacted the ground, the cap fired. My pocket money had all gone. I wanted it. Desperately wanted it.

I saw myself taking it, sliding it inside my jacket and leaving the store, looking guiltily left, right, above, behind until I got home and could examine my loot. God! He was making me remember the days and days of anguish, waiting for Mr Duke to come knocking on the door to take me away to the police station. I felt the awful reality of my crime, the sickness in my stomach worrying about being found out. He showed me the many occasions I'd walked past that store. Six months before I dared to enter it and, even then, I was in fear of a hand on my shoulder, 'Got you, you little *thief*!' Perhaps that I wasn't caught was one of the reasons I'd ever since had a great sense of fairness and justice.

No, *no*! ***No!*** That's mine! Not yours – ***mine!*** He'd found another memory, on board the Gateway, precious time with Linda after our frantic departure from the moon. Oh, so real. It *was* real! God, I was actually feeling every sensation of the tangling of our naked limbs and bodies during our freefall lovemaking tango. I relived the actual instant which had created another entity, a human one which was growing inside Linda's womb at this very moment. It was more than a memory. It was as if it was happening again now. No, no, I told him, these were my intimate memories, not for sharing. I was aware of an astonishing erection. ***Stop!*** He stopped at my request… eventually. I laughed at my embarrassment and was shocked that he could see such things, and that they could cause such reactions, but also staggered that these memories were so easy to recall, and in such detail. Frighteningly lovely.

I fought off his desire to find out more. I supposed he'd be with me in future during intimate moments. Could I ask him to leave me and sit on the bedside table as one did with spectacles? I laughed at the thought. But he was searching out other sexual memories. My disastrous loss of virginity and, oh no, he'd found memories of me with Penny Heston! Stop right there!

'***Stop!***' I shouted at full voice. I really didn't want to remember anything about my infidelity. It had almost cost me Linda. He did stop and withdrew from that part of my mind. I told him there were certain memories which were mine and mine alone and he could look if he wished, but I didn't want to see them with him. I wondered if that was even possible. I guessed we'd have to learn and set our own rules. We must establish boundaries for each other.

The next three hours were fascinating as my mind became able to use its new faculties to assess the difficult situation we were in at Moonbase. The clarity of vision gave me hope that I could find a way through the political and strategic mess which was threatening to engulf us.

I told the entity to shut up. He did. He stopped rummaging. I allowed my thoughts to settle down. I had to Skype Linda and I didn't know how I was going to explain what I'd done. With my entity promising to retreat into silence, I made the call.

‘Hi, darling,’ she said. ‘Why the encrypted channel?’

‘Don’t want to be listened into. How’s my son?’ I said and waited for the interminable three seconds to pass.

‘Or daughter,’ she said. ‘Scan tomorrow. Do you want to know?’

‘No, I’ll wait for the surprise. Have you got a piece of paper there?’

‘Yes.’ She reached for a pad.

‘Don’t say them aloud in case our voices are still being listened to, but copy down these coordinates then show them back to me so I can check them,’ I said, holding up the note which Roy had given me.

I checked that she had an accurate copy. ‘Put them in your cloud storage. Give the handwritten version to our lawyer in a sealed envelope to be given to that New York Times guy you know, don’t say his name, in the event of my death.’

‘Death? *Death?* What? What’s going on? Why do we need them? Why are they so important? What’s all this about?’

‘They’re moon coordinates. We need to keep them safe.’

‘You sound a little different. Are you okay?’ she said. ‘Mark, you’re worrying me.’

She was always very intuitive. ‘I have something to tell you, and I don’t know how to do it,’ I said.

‘Start at the beginning,’ she said, and I began the most difficult explanation I have ever had to make. Fortunately, I had an alien genius inside me to offer help, comfort, concentration and an improved empathy and insight into life.

The last few minutes of the Skype call was a series of searching questions to me. Linda was satisfying herself that it really was me. I let him take control so that she could ask him about the symbiosis. She saw my eyes change and I showed her that I could retain, or handover control any time I wished. I hoped she believed me as it was crucial. She assured me she did. I even had the entity leave me and sit on a calculator, then return to me through the back of my hand.

When our call finished, I turned off the lights and my entity closed my eyes for me, helped me blank my mind, lowered my temperature and slowed my heartbeat. So began a deep, dreamless and amazingly restful sleep.

While I slept, he opened and closed the filing cabinets of my mind. By dawn he really did know me.

24 Last Chance Saloon

At breakfast, I met up with Bill and Anna.

'Any second thoughts?' I asked.

'Not from me,' said Bill.

'Nor me,' said Anna.

'Come to my cabin when you finish here,' I said.

∞∞∞∞∞∞∞∞∞∞

I had to find out what their true thoughts were about what we were about to do. We were planning to obstruct the military. Were we right or wrong to do that? If this were to go wrong, we'd never be allowed to work for NASA again, in fact, we could be imprisoned for life if it were seen as treason.

They entered my cabin. I held the metal box Roy had given me. It still contained two entities. I asked mine to leave me and join them. He didn't want to, and I didn't want him to leave either, but I insisted he must leave if we were to be convinced it was not a parasitic takeover. Reluctantly he joined the others.

Bill and Anna, with puzzled expressions, watched my entity leave my hand and make its way into the container.

'Right. You two do the same,' I said.

'Why?' asked Anna.

'Because it is an order,' I said.

She looked at me severely, then shrugged. Her entity emerged from her palm and joined the others in the box.

'Bill?' I said.

‘I need to know why?’ he said.

‘You and Anna are my most intimate advisers and I am asking you to do so. Trust me,’ I said unemotionally.

He frowned, turned his hand over and I saw it drop into the container. ‘Here you are then,’ he said.

‘Do you want this too?’ asked Anna.

‘What?’ I asked looking at her open palm.

A second entity emerged from her skin, very slightly smaller, but fully formed.

‘It reproduced inside you?’ I asked.

‘She did.’

The smaller entity joined the others in the box, and I closed the lid. I crouched to open my personal wall safe and slid the container into the small space inside, which also contained a few private items.

I slammed the door shut, stood and said, ‘Come with me.’

I’d already checked with the computer that the bio dome was clear of people and we set off along the main corridor, down the tunnel which ran past the surgery, and into the amazing bio dome with its small area of developing woodland, shrubs, grasses and wildflowers. Bees continued their tiny lives, buzzing in and out of flowers. I led my colleagues along the left central pathway to the chicken compound where our feathered friends were clucking away as they dug around in the soil imported from a world some two hundred and fifty thousand miles away.

We got to the bench beside them and I sat, waving Bill and Anna to join me.

'Well, Mark, spill it,' said Bill.

'I needed to talk to you without the influence of the entities or our bosses at NASA and the military men pulling the strings which separate them from us but bind them to each other.

'We don't know yet,' I said, 'but I feel that we are almost certainly going to take a treasonous route within the next couple of days. We all need to *own* what we're doing. Are we about to betray humanity? There is no one to blame but us – not the entities, not Roy, not NASA nor the military. How do you feel about it? Anna, you first.'

'One thing I do know, Mark, is that I'd rather have my entity helping me to answer your question,' she said.

'That would obviously defeat the purpose,' I said.

'Yes. I see that. Okay,' she began and took a deep breath, 'the entities are a game changer. With them we have the opportunity to improve our intellect, our intelligence, our compassion and our health. Last night, my entity found a cancer growing in my oesophagus.'

'No!' Bill said.

'Yes. And it throttled off the blood vessels. She tells me the cancer will die and then just be cleared out of my system naturally. Just that alone is a reason to unite with them. Imagine all of the people in the world who will be saved. No more high blood pressure, diabetes, motor neurone disease, Parkinson's, obesity, dementia, infectious diseases. All gone. No more worries about antibiotics either. Our biggest problem then will be overpopulation, but they can even help with that! No more unplanned pregnancies and they can help us control our numbers in future.'

'That's not an advantage I'd considered. It has killed your cancer?' I said.

'Yes. Will be gone in a week or so. How can we possibly deny this symbiosis? It is the most wonderful thing that has ever happened to humankind. She also told me that I'd live much longer with her looking after me. My remaining lifespan could be doubled.'

'Bill?'

'Even without knowing the health benefits, I could not, knowingly, allow these creatures to be exterminated. So, a flat out "no" from me. We must protect them,' Bill said. 'They must be saved.'

'Yes. I agree, but I had to check with you. We're definitely not still under their influence?'

'No, there's a bloody big gap where his influence should be, and I want him back in it!' said Bill.

'Same with me. We're with you, Mark,' said Anna.

'Both of us. One hundred per cent. We must protect them,' said Bill.

We returned to my cabin and collected our alien partners.

25 Asimov Rille

In the com dome, late morning, I confirmed to Neil that we were planning to visit the rille with a guaranteed safe passage from Roy. He was concerned but gave me a go.

Thirty minutes later we had a firm plan for the visit. Roy would collect Bill, Anna and myself at eleven. I needed to speak with Doug without giving away that I was now a host to an entity. I used my new talent to speak mentally to my entity and told him that he must remain totally inactive during my meeting.

Doug had made his military HQ in a side room off the rec dome. As I walked in, I could see him at the far side, throwing darts at the dartboard.

I grabbed a set and we took turns to throw.

I said, 'Neil has given Bill, Anna and I permission to visit the rille under a guarantee of safe passage from Roy.'

'I'll get Mike and another Marine to accompany you.'

'No. We need to be alone inside the rille,' I said.

'Wow, Mark! That's the second hundred plus score you've thrown in a row!' said Doug.

'My lucky day,' I said, ensuring my newly found accuracy was suppressed. I threw a couple of twenty-sixes and a forty-five to try to defuse suspicion.

'I don't like it,' he said.

What did he mean? Had he guessed from my sudden new skill with darts?

He continued, 'Take a couple of my men with you as bodyguards. I promise they'll melt into the background, but if there's any attempt to take you over, they can react and irradiate everyone.'

Phew! My high darts scores hadn't given me away. 'They won't let us in with a projector but I can understand your concern. You can always check us when we return,' I said.

I would have to find a way of protecting us if we were to be irradiated. Either that or we'd have to leave our entities in the rille. Roy had told me not to be too concerned about it, which just added to the mystery. He must have something in mind.

'Okay, but I'll have a squad at the entrance in our buggy,' he said.

He put down his darts, walked into his room and returned with a small clip-on microphone and an architectol – a 3D scanning device.

'Take this scanner. We might as well get some intel. You can also wear this mike; use it to let us know if you need help. This is the switch which turns it on,' Doug said, handing over the architectol and pointing out the switch on the collar microphone.

I turned them over in my fingers and popped them into my pocket. 'Okay, Doug. Sounds like a plan.'

It took Doug eight attempts to hit the winning double while I was contriving to miss double one by not too great a margin.

∞∞∞∞∞∞∞∞∞∞∞∞

‘I still don’t like this,’ said Doug over the radio.

I stood on the regolith in a lightweight EVA suit together with Anna and Bill. In the distance, buggy one was approaching.

‘We’ll be okay, Doug,’ I said. ‘I’m wearing the mike and will turn it on if we feel threatened in the slightest. Your squad will be in buggy three, yes?’

‘Yes,’ he said. ‘We’ll follow you to the rille and will be waiting outside.

‘Copy that, Doug,’ I said.

Buggy one pulled up beside us. I climbed the ladder and entered the rear section of the familiar vehicle with the others following closely behind. I could see Roy in the front section without a helmet. I closed the hatch, checked the seals and said, ‘Selena, pressurise the aft section.’

‘Pressurising the aft section, Mark,’ said buggy one’s computer.

Once pressurised, Roy said, ‘Welcome aboard.’

The buggy turned and headed off across the surface of the moon. Once again that thrill of knowing where we were and staring at the magnificent desolation, as Aldrin had once described it.

‘Why did you want me to bring the entities in the box? They’d have been perfectly secure in my cabin safe. In fact, there are now three. Anna’s reproduced,’ I said.

‘Tosh wants them. He’ll explain,’ said Roy. ‘How’re you getting on with them?’

He was answered with a chorus of ‘Fine!’ from all three of us.

‘Did you get any response from the universities?’

‘No. Neil said they wanted more time,’ I said. ‘Can you tell us more about what you’re doing in the rille? We understand it has to do with unifying quantum gravity with relativity.’

‘Well, it’s more to do with what that means to us in terms of astrophysics and spaceflight. I’ll leave it to Mary to explain. She’s the astrophysics genius. Have you experienced the clearer thinking you now have with your entities?’

‘Yes,’ I said, moving forward and slotting myself into the right cockpit seat. ‘You couldn’t save Blake?’

‘No. I managed to reseal his faceplate. He did regain consciousness back at Moonbase when Tosh pumped some adrenaline into him, but smashing his faceplate irreparably damaged his lungs, beyond even the ability of his entity to repair.’

‘I feel dreadful that I killed him,’ I said.

‘You almost killed both of us.’

‘Presumably you got clear of the blast somehow.’

‘Yes,’ said Roy. ‘Blake falling knocked me off the Dragonstar ladder. I bounced to my feet, grabbed Blake and pulled him clear as you took off.’

'Very lucky,' I said.

'Well, you must remember that Dragonstar launch motors have little more power than a hovercraft. I'm not sure they'd do much damage unless you were directly beneath them,' explained Roy. 'Moon-landing deniers used to claim there was no blast crater visible under the Apollos, but, of course, the engines were never powerful enough to create a blast crater. Ignorance was always the conspiracists' ally.' I nodded agreement. 'Nevertheless, being hit by the direct blast would not have been good for my health.'

The Asimov Rille was soon directly ahead. Roy turned buggy one so that it was square on to the cave entrance. 'Helmets on and secure,' he said fitting his own helmet as the three of us attached ours. The lightweight suits had a two-hour air supply so were nowhere near as bulky as the main moon EVA suits.

We all checked each other's helmet seals and climbed down onto the surface of the moon. I turned and looked in the direction of Moonbase and could see buggy three approaching through lengthening shadows as the moon's fourteen days of daylight slowly approached their end.

We entered the cave.

'Fascinating tunnel,' I said over the radio.

'Yes, when this is all over, I'd like to write a paper on this one. You saw that it branches?' said Roy.

'I did. Quite a surprise.'

'Indeed. It also has a large cavern.'

'Really?'

'Yes,' said Roy. 'You'll see soon enough.'

We made our way down the gentle slope, came to the junction and continued along the left passage.

'Longer than I expected,' Bill said.

'Yes, we were surprised, but, as you'll see, there's an even bigger surprise at the end,' said Roy.

We followed a gentle curve to the left until we reached the airlock, seamlessly built into the tunnel and surrounded by aluminium sheets set into the walls. Roy pressed the green button and the air began to cycle.

'What are you using for power?' I asked.

'We're using the hydrogen generator.'

'Regolith providing the H_20?'

'No. At the end of the rille we found a frozen water source. As the rille warmed we're able to tap it. That provides our oxygen and surplus hydrogen for the generator. Works fine,' said Roy.

'Impressive,' I said.

It took two or three minutes for the air to be extracted. The "augmented" or "enhanced" humans, descriptions I preferred to "infected", would not have air to waste even if they had found a water source. I was sure they would be very carefully preserving their resources.

Roy swung the door open and the four of us entered. It was a tight space. Four was about the maximum who could use this airlock at any one time. Roy pulled the door shut behind us. The inner airlock door was a mirror image. He hit the green button and the atmosphere flooded into the space, causing our lightweight spacesuits to deflate. A chime sounded; Roy removed his helmet and the rest of us followed his lead. The inner door opened.

We were greeted by a smiling Tosh and Jenny. We all hugged, and it was special for me because I hadn't seen them since I'd fled Moonbase with Linda.

'Tosh, Jenny, so good to see you,' I said, finally escaping Tosh's bear hug.

'How are you getting on with your little friends?' he asked.

'Fine, so far,' I said.

'Yes, no problems,' said Bill.

'Wonderful,' said Anna. 'I've been hosting the longest and it just gets better.'

'Yes, it does, doesn't it?' said Jenny.

'Get those suits off and come through,' said Tosh as he set off along more of the tunnel with Jenny, leaving extra space for the four of us to remove the suits.

The tunnel didn't look any different. It measured about two point five metres in diameter. It was dark and had rippled walls from the time when lava would have forced its way out and onto the moon's surface. LED lights every few metres led us deeper into the moon. It was good to feel the texture with my fingers. It was so smooth it seemed to have been fused by the volcanic heat all those millions of years before, but with broken bubbles leaving myriad small and large hollows in its surface.

'Plenty of time to study the rock in the future,' said Roy as he led us further into the depths of the moon.

The journey was so like Cavor, Bedford and Kate's experience with the Selenites and I wondered if, at any moment, one of HG Wells' fanciful invented creatures would appear coming the other way. As it was, we were accompanying real aliens towards their lair. We were, in fact, also part alien now. Frivolously, I wondered if we should call ourselves the Selenites.

Roy stopped about fifty metres in and turned. The tunnel had developed a lip and he was climbing down a ladder.

'Eight rungs,' he said. 'We've put silicone on them so you shouldn't slip.'

As I got to the lip, I looked forward in amazement. We were entering a huge cavern. The other side was at least thirty metres away. I looked up and it extended five metres in that direction. LED lamps had been installed and they lit the interior. At the bottom, the augmented humans had excavated the curved surface into a flat area on which they lived and worked. The tunnel continued downwards through the wall on the far side.

I was surprised how quickly I saw and, more importantly, absorbed what I was seeing. My entity was obviously helping me interpret the scene. A clearly defined medical centre stood on one side. Adjacent to it was a large area with cooking facilities for relaxing and socialising. A small anonymous structure to the right beneath us was probably the bathroom. It was clearly a home from home, a veritable mini-Moonbase.

I turned and climbed down the ladder. The others were all waiting for us – Crystal, Jenny, Tosh, Mary and Roy. It was wonderful to see them all again because I'd imagined that they might all be dead, or some sort of living-dead, controlled by the alien entities.

Introductions were made for Bill and Anna, then Tosh asked us to come through to the socialising area and we all found somewhere to sit. There were not enough seats, but we were offered what was available, and the original augmented humans sat on chair arms or the floor.

I felt compelled to say something. 'I'm impressed by your layout here. Looks very efficient.'

'We had to make the best of a bad job, Mark,' said Tosh. 'We considered moving to Ben Lei, the Chinese habitat, but felt we could protect ourselves better here.'

'Yes, sound decision,' said Bill. 'But you can't survive a sustained military attack or even a siege.'

'We know that,' he snapped in his usual bad-tempered manner. 'We've not been twiddling our thumbs, you know. We've spent all of this time learning about ourselves and our enhanced abilities and how they can help us.'

'What's this about quantum gravity and general relativity?' asked Anna.

'Later. For now, we have work to do,' said Tosh. 'I need all of your entities on this tray, please.'

'Why?' I asked, shocked and, I must admit, reluctant to hand him over.

'I'm the doctor and I need them!' said Tosh angrily. He always had been an impatient individual and hated having his medical authority challenged. I suppose it was nice to see that his entity hadn't changed his underlying character. He really was the same old Tosh.

'Calm down, Tosh,' said Roy.

'Calm down? Don't tell me to calm down! I need to get this done,' he said, raising his voice. 'Those bastards could come to eradicate us any moment!'

'Give him your entities,' Roy said, taking the tray from the doctor and passing it to me. 'He needs to vaccinate them.'

My entity exited to the tray and I passed it to Bill. 'Vaccinate from what?' I asked.

'It's *not* a vaccination,' scoffed Tosh, loudly. 'I am adding a chemical to them which is absorbed into their outer skin to prevent them being damaged by your damned *Star Trek* ray guns! They'll build up resistance over the coming days but should be fine against your current version.'

He took the tray and the box which contained the other three and disappeared into his medical area. I felt hollow without him. It was like a mild depression, a hopelessness. The second time in a single day. My goodness, I realised what Crystal must have been experiencing for those two days. I wanted him back. I needed him!

'What about the ones you put in the secret location?' I asked.

'Already done,' said Jenny. 'Crys and I buried them again this morning.'

'Does this mean you will no longer be affected by the radiation projectors, or the ray guns as Tosh so accurately describes them?'

'Not just "we",' Roy said. 'You too.'

'I see,' I said. 'I was thinking we'd have to leave them behind as we're sure to be irradiated when we get back to Moonbase.'

'Tosh reckons they'll be fine for up to twenty seconds,' said Roy.

'It should be around half that as there's been a directive from NASA saying we need to minimise unnecessary human exposure,' I said.

Mary said, 'Was it the Van Allen belts?'

They knew! 'How do you mean?' I said, playing dumb.

'Don't be daft, Mark, this is enhanced humans you are talking to' said Roy. 'One of the entities went to Earth with you and Linda. At some point it *will* have escaped. We don't think you'd have had one of these then.' He held up the outer case of a disassembled projector they must have stolen from somewhere. It explained how they'd learned their range and how to create a method of protecting themselves.

'No, we didn't have them,' I said.

'Well, what happened to it?' asked Roy. 'The only solution we could think of is the Van Allen belts.'

Was there any point in trying to hide the truth now? 'Yes, it was the inner Van Allen belt. The entity had infected me. Linda actually tried to crash the Orion, but it was too late, already on automatic approach. It died before we got into the atmosphere.'

'See?' said Tosh re-emerging with the tray. 'Told you that was the only way it could have died. Here's your entities back.'

'Did you *really* try to kill yourselves?' asked Jenny.

'Linda tried to sabotage re-entry, but the Orion had already switched to autonomous re-entry mode,' I said.

'Just offer the backs of your hands. They'll know which of you belongs to them,' said Tosh.

'I'd rather think of him belonging to me,' I said.

'Delude yourself then, but I can assure you that *they* are the primary partner in the symbiosis,' said Tosh.

Was he right? Did I want this? I'd thought I was in charge, but if my entity was, it was still arguable that this was a takeover.

'What's the problem, Mark?' asked Roy.

'I didn't think I was subsidiary to him,' I said. 'I thought we were equal partners.'

'Ignore Tosh,' said Roy. 'Control is equal.'

'Human egos!' huffed Tosh. 'It's all semantics.'

He was right, of course. I offered my hand to the tray. One jumped across to me and I was no longer alone. I was whole again!

'Did Linda come with you?' asked Jenny. 'How is she?'

'She's fine,' I said. 'Expecting, so grounded.'

'Yours, I guess?' said Roy.

'Yes. We married too.'

'Congratulations,' said Jenny jumping up and down.

Crystal came across and gave me a hug and I got a kiss on the cheek from Mary.

'Congrats, mate,' said Roy shaking my hand.

'Teach you to be more damn careful next time!' shouted Tosh as he returned the tray to his lab area.

It was all so natural. Nothing alien about any of them. They were just how I remembered them.

I asked, 'What's this gravity thing? NASA haven't come back with anything from the two universities you suggested.'

'It could take a day or two for them to even realise what they've been given,' said Mary.

'What is it?' I asked again.

'Even in your now enhanced condition,' said Mary, 'it would take some time before you'd understand.'

'Do your best,' I said.

'Dark matter has been hidden from us despite the best efforts of the Large Hadron Collider,' explained Mary, sitting back into one of the easy chairs which I recognised as missing from the rec dome. 'Through quantum interaction, it is the dark matter which has prevented physicists linking quantum gravity with relativity. It just couldn't be understood without taking into account the additional mass of dark matter and its hidden behaviour in our non-quantum universe.'

'And?' said Bill as Mary paused.

'Patience. None of it is easy, Bill. Despite our enhanced intellects, it is still complex science for us too,' she said. 'In the simplest of terms, imagine an object sitting in space, like this pawn. You might want to push it to another location, like this.'

She pushed the pawn and it moved across the surface of the chess board on the table.

'If I push it here, it moves this way. If I push it here, it moves in a different direction. So, if I know where I want it to be, using the correct amount of force, I can move it to that position.'

'Obviously,' Bill said.

'Well, this is not so obvious – what if I wanted to push it to mission control in Houston?'

Bill said, 'You'd put it in a Dragonstar, transfer it to an Orion, collect it from splashdown and put it in a plane to take it to Houston.'

'You're correct, I could use that method,' said Mary, 'but there's an easier way. If I give it a quantum shove, it will move through the quantum universe and arrive instantly in Houston. Actually, the quantum shove is more of a quantum *pull* than a push. It *pulls* Houston here as if we'd reached out and grabbed it, temporarily stretching a piece of the end location so that it sits beside this location. Imagine a map of the USA on cloth. Now imagine reaching out to it, pinching Houston between your fingers and pulling it towards you. In simple terms, that is what we can do.' She tapped the pawn. 'Then that tiny, minimal energy shove, sees it complete the journey in no time at all,' and she flicked the pawn across the board and it tumbled onto the table.

'Crazy!' said Bill.

'You're trying to understand it without all the background learning. Of course it seems crazy to you, Bill.' Mary sat forward in the chair. Bill went to speak but she put out her hand to stop him.

'Analogies can only offer a little help, but I'd like you to think about Galileo, who had proven to his own satisfaction that the moons of Jupiter revolved around the giant planet and the Earth revolved around the sun. The Church, in its usual ultimate wisdom, said that Galileo was blaspheming because the sun, quite clearly, revolves around the Earth which was solid and motionless at the centre of the universe. Galileo recanted to save himself, but that did not change the fact that Earth *does* revolve around the sun. Similarly, your cry of "Crazy!" does not change the fact that a quantum push would send this pawn to Houston.

'Galileo is supposed to have admitted that the Earth was a solid world in the centre of the universe to save his neck. An apocryphal account tells us that he said, "Eppur si muove" or "Albeit does move" when he left court. Let me tell you in modern English, Bill – it *would* arrive in Houston!'

'Show me?' Bill challenged.

'We don't have the equipment to do it, only the proof that it can be done,' she said.

'I suppose,' I said, 'if you can do it with the pawn, you'd be able to do it with a spaceship?'

'Yes. It is dependent on a number of factors including the amount of energy which is introduced to the system, and the mass of the object, but, yes, it could be done with a spaceship. Want to go to see all those exoplanets we've found orbiting other stars, Mark? No longer impossible,' Mary said.

'What equipment would you need to demonstrate it?' asked Anna.

'We don't have the main components available on the moon,' said Mary. 'Only the Earth can build what we need, but they won't know how to do it without our help. We've given them the maths, but not the ability to make use of it. They need us for that!'

'Are there other uses?' I asked.

‘There will be thousands, but another one which we have been trying to produce is the transport system used in *Star Trek*,’ said Mary.

‘But that’s been proven to be ridiculous, breaking the body down and transmitting it. That really *is* crazy!’ said Anna.

‘Yes, it is the way you describe it,’ said Mary. ‘But what if I gave a quantum shove to you, Anna? You’d instantly be in Houston!’

‘*Really*?’ I said.

‘In theory, yes,’ said Tosh. ‘But we’ll need to test it. We need to test all of it, but a bunch of backward humans are likely to wipe us out before we can!’

26 What Next?

When we emerged from Asimov Rille, four Marines, together with Doug, were standing on the surface, apparently waiting, although we knew they must have heard what we were saying once we'd suited up at the airlock. Our suit radios were on an open channel deliberately. We carefully chatted so as only to give away what we wanted them to hear.

As we boarded buggy one, we saw Doug's men making their way hurriedly back to buggy three. They turned and headed towards Moonbase.

We drove more slowly, talking about options for survival.

'What do you think Earth will do?' asked Roy.

'I honestly don't know,' I said.

'If I were them,' said Bill, 'I'd wait for our report of the visit to the rille before acting. That should mean we are safe for the time being, but that might only be twenty-four hours.'

Anna said, 'I hate the concept that we are now the enemy. We must find a way to convince Earth that the entities are working with us.'

'They won't believe it,' said Bill.

'Well, we did,' I said.

'Not initially,' said Roy.

‘Come on, Roy,’ I said, ‘that was entirely your fault by sending in that force to attack us. It wasn’t a very “enhanced” thing to do, was it?’

‘It would’ve been if we’d succeeded,’ said Roy, ‘and, damn it, we almost did. From what you say, we were only an instant or two from taking over you and Doug. Frankly that would’ve been *it*. The medical team wouldn’t have stood a chance if we already had everybody else.’

‘No. I suppose it was a near thing,’ I said.

‘You’re right,’ said Anna.

‘Once we’ve reported, what will their next move be?’ Bill asked.

‘Either they’ll want to send a group to study the augmented or they’ll give an order to Doug to obliterate you,’ I said. ‘And it might all come down to how convincing I can be.’

‘You might convince Neil,’ said Anna, ‘but not the generals. They’ll be paranoid.’

‘We’ll see.’

Moonbase was now visible. We had minutes before we’d have to leave Roy. Just before I put on my helmet I said to him, ‘I’ll try to let you know what’s happening.’ Roy gave me a thumbs-up and I closed the airtight cockpit panel. We asked Selena to evacuate the air.

Soon, we stood on the regolith outside the garage dome and were making our way inside. Doug and two Marines were waiting.

‘Wait there please, Mark,’ said Doug as the main door slid downwards, a seal was made and the pumps started to pressurise the garage dome.

I could see more Marines cleaning the invasive regolith off buggy three. An unpleasant, but essential task. The dust got everywhere.

Pressure reached normal and we all removed our helmets.

‘Hold still,’ said Doug. ‘We’re going to irradiate you. Sorry. Can’t take the chance you’ve picked up any little passengers.

‘Okay, Doug, but keep it to the minimum. NASA are worried about its effect on the human body,’ I said. My entity was anxious. He was relying on an argumentative and opinionated human doctor to have resolved the radiation problem.

The Marines used their projectors for about ten seconds, which we knew was enough to kill the entities.

How are you? I thought and the answer came back immediately. *Sick, but I’ll be okay.* Tosh’s vaccine had worked its miracle.

I looked at Anna and Bill who seemed well too.

‘All clear, Mark. You can de-suit,’ said Doug.

His two armed Marines went on to do other work in the garage dome while we all stripped out of our suits.

‘So, what did you learn?’ asked Doug.

‘They’re seriously mentally enhanced, Doug,’ said Anna.

‘We’re going to suggest to NASA, that there is experimentation with the LRPs to try to find out the limits of their powers,’ I said. ‘As soon as I’m out of this gear, I’m going to call Neil.’

‘Okay. Can I sit in?’ Doug asked.

‘No problem. Join me when you’re out of that suit,’ I said and, with Anna and Bill, I headed towards the com dome. Doug had on a full EVA suit, so it would be a few minutes before he would come through to join us.

∞∞∞∞∞∞∞∞∞∞∞

‘And that’s more or less it, Neil,’ I said. ‘Bill, Anna and I are convinced the LRPs are no longer oppressing their hosts. All of the infected were perfectly in control of their own bodies and minds. The enhancements are, apparently, incredible, and none of them want to return to ordinary life. Over.’

‘How can we trust them? Over,’ asked General Gilby.

‘How can anyone trust anybody? Over,’ I said.

‘What are you suggesting, Mark? Over,’ asked Neil.

‘I think we should carry out studies under controlled conditions where some of us and some of them work with and without the LRPs. We could set it up in part of the bio dome,’ I said.

Bill added, ‘We could film it all and you can watch the results down there.’

‘What did the universities say about the material Anna sent you? Over,’ I asked.

‘Amherst was suspicious. Cambridge were excited, but neither college fully understood what was being proposed. Over,’ said Neil.

‘If we were studying them here, the scientists could speak to them directly and get answers or explanations in real time. Over,’ I said.

‘Thanks, Mark. We’ll think about it. Over,’ said Neil.

‘Let me emphasise once again, in the strongest possible terms, that Bill, Anna and I are absolutely convinced that these are intelligent beings and that they are no longer a threat to the human race. We should treat them as such and not as enemies. Over,’ I said.

‘Okay, Mark. We understand your viewpoint. Over,’ said Neil.

‘Okay, Neil. Let us know sooner rather than later, please. Over.’

‘Will do. Out.’

∞∞∞∞∞∞∞∞∞∞∞∞

Bill, Anna and I had dinner together, keeping our conversation at a low level. It was remarkable that no one realised that we’d been augmented. It clearly showed we were in control, not the entities.

That evening and night, we learned more about our new abilities and dug even deeper into our memories. The entities found the tiniest crevices of our minds, pulling to the surface everything we had ever learned. I marvelled at my ability to understand geological features from my masters and PhD, which had previously eluded me or seemed of little importance. I could only guess at the effect this would have on someone like Mary, who was already an astrophysics genius. What sort of effect would the symbiosis have had on someone like Einstein or Hawking?

This was far too great an opportunity for humanity. It mustn't be lost through the paranoia of military chiefs or failure to properly study the augmented humans. I went to see Krishna. It was time we had more allies.

27 Betrayal

I walked into the common room for breakfast and immediately noticed the lack of people. This was the one time of the day when the place was usually crowded. Pete and Penny were sitting at one table, Krishna and one of his nurses, Jack, at another. Anna was eating by the panoramic window and Bill was cooking himself something.

That was everyone.

I joined Bill and made myself some toast, coffee and a bowl of muesli. We joined Anna.

'Strangely quiet,' I said.

'Yes. Too quiet,' said Anna.

Bill used his personal intercom, 'Computer. Where is Doug?'

'Doug is not in Moonbase, Bill,' said the computer.

'Computer, how many people are in Moonbase?' I asked.

'There are currently fifteen people in Moonbase, Mark'

'There's something going on,' I said. 'I'm going to the com dome.'

All three of us jumped up, hurrying out of the common room and into the com dome. Dave Morgan was at the console.

'What's going on?' I asked.

'The Marines are heading for the rille,' he said. 'Didn't you know?'

'No, we most certainly *did **not** know*!' said Bill.

'What's happening? Tell us what you know,' I said.

'Doug and Mike were talking to Earth earlier and I heard them being authorised to carryout "Operation Free Minds",' said Dave. 'They left and there was a lot of activity in the garage dome. About thirty minutes ago, all three buggies left. The open buggies were well overloaded, and the main buggy was towing a trailer with more Marines and what looked like weapons.'

'Unbelievable,' said Anna. 'How dare they?'

'I thought you knew, Mark. Sorry,' said Dave.

'Get me mission control,' I said, and Dave busied himself with the transmitter controls.

'That's you connected, Mark.'

'Sorry, Dave. Can we ask you to leave the com dome?' asked Anna.

'Yes. I'll be in the common room,' he said.

'Thanks, Dave,' said Bill.

'Neil?'

'Good morning, Mark.'

'*What the fuck is going on*?'

'Sorry, Mark. It was a strategic military decision,' Neil said. 'They would not allow me to even tell you.'

God. The communication delay was frustrating. 'Explain,' I said. 'Why wasn't I informed or even consulted?'

'This wasn't me, Mark. The generals took over mission control and gave the orders.'

'What are the orders?'

'To take the Asimov Rille and bring the infected back to Moonbase where they'll be irradiated.'

I couldn't believe it. 'The symbiosis is incredible, Neil. They've even given us warp travel. Hurt them and we lose it all. They are no longer a threat. Haven't the universities got back to you?'

'Yes, but the military weren't interested. Cambridge said the material was ground-breaking. Amherst's scepticism had gone and they wanted to know more,' said Neil.

'This is crazy, Neil. It's genocide!' I exclaimed.

'They don't see it like that. They see these things as bugs or viruses, not intelligent beings.'

'But they add to our intelligence exponentially. If they're harmed it will be the world's most stupid decision ever,' I said.

'NASA agrees with you to a degree and wanted to carry out the study you suggested, but we were overruled.'

'Out, Neil,' I said then tuned the console to channel sixteen.

'Roy, come in, over,' I said.

It was twenty or thirty seconds before there was a reply, 'Hi, Mark. Roy here.'

'You're under attack or soon will be,' I said.

'Yes, we know,' said Roy. 'Some of them are in the airlock now. We're not going to resist. Presumably they'll irradiate us and then bring us back with them. We'll play dead. Did you deal with Krishna?'

'Yes, and both the nurses,' I said.

'What's this about?' asked Anna.

'Okay, Mark. Don't worry about us. The airlock is cycling, bye,' Roy said, and the carrier wave dropped to silent.

'What were you saying about Krishna and the nurses?' asked Bill.

'I was going to tell you over breakfast. I gave them the other entities from the box and sat with them until they stopped resisting and I could explain their symbiotic nature,' I said.

'And they went along with it?' asked Anna.

'They are with us now. Computer, where is Krishna?' I said.

'Krishna is in the surgery, Mark.'

'NASA calling Moonbase, over,' Neil's voice came from the console.

'Not in the mood for chitchat,' I said to him.

‘We need to talk, Mark. I had no choice in this,’ said Neil.

‘Later, maybe. I’m busy right now… *trying* to prevent *genocide! Mark out!*’ I said angrily and cut the connection. ‘Come on,’ I said to Bill and Anna, ‘let’s go to the surgery.’

∞∞∞∞∞∞∞∞∞∞∞

We stood in ward two with Krishna, Diana and Jack. I explained that an attack on the rille was in progress.

‘How are you getting on with your entities?’ asked Anna.

‘Amazing,’ said Jack. ‘I couldn’t believe Mark had infected us deliberately, but then it, he, showed me how the connection works.’

‘My entity says he is ready to divide,’ I said.

‘Mine too,’ said Bill.

We sat down and watched our hands as duplicates eased their way out of our flesh and collected on a kidney dish.

‘Computer, ask Pete to come to the surgery,’ I said.

‘Pete is being asked to come to the surgery, Mark,’ said the computer.

Krishna opened the ward door and said, ‘Alexei, when Pete arrives, will you bring him in here, please.’

A few minutes later, the door opened and they both came into ward two.

‘Please sit down,’ I said, and they sat on one of the couches.

‘Please don’t panic,’ I said and both men looked at me suspiciously.

Bill stood before them with the kidney dish and they saw what it contained. Alexei didn’t have time to react, but Pete did. He tried to knock the dish away, but his fight ceased as the entity brought him under control.

‘Sit still,’ I said, seeing the glazed eyes within their frightened expressions.

‘Release them,’ I said and watched as they returned to normal but looked at the rest of us in disbelief.

‘You’ve infected us. You bastards!’ shouted Pete.

‘Settle down. Relax,’ said Krishna. ‘Takeover it isn’t; symbiosis it is. Let your new friend show you its wonders. Offers nothing but good things, it does. Certainly, won’t hurt you.’

Now there were eight of us. If things went well, we’d reclaim control of Moonbase. We’d certainly crossed a line. There was no longer any turning back.

∞∞∞∞∞∞∞∞∞∞

I sat in the com dome watching the door close now that all the buggies were inside. Red stripes on Doug’s suit shoulders identified him as the senior officer. Mike’s insignia were blue as second in command.

They stood, with eight Marines guarding the prisoners as they exited the buggies. Four others were already vacuuming the outsides of the buggies. Then they were instructed to vacuum the prisoners' and Marines' suits. Procedures had to be followed, even in this bizarre scenario. The infected were lined up and the projectors used to irradiate them. All five fell to the ground as if dead. The Marines helped them to their feet.

'You'll have bad headaches for a while until we can get these things out of you in the surgery. Ah, here's Diana,' said Doug as the nurse entered the garage dome.

'I know you're hurting but come with me and we'll soon have you back to normal,' she said.

The prisoners, all holding their heads, followed the nurse out of the dome.

'Right,' said Doug, 'I want this place and the inside of those buggies as dust free as a microchip factory, in double quick time!'

In the surgery, the augmented discontinued their feigned headaches and many more entities climbed out of their suits and into a storage flask.

'Doug and Mike, please make your way to the surgery,' said the computer.

I heard the message and knew we'd have two more recruits in quick order. By mid-afternoon we'd all be Selenites.

28 Control

Doug, Anna, Bill and I sat around the main console in the com dome.

'Receiving you, over,' said Neil.

'Mark here. Well, it's done. The military have won. It was a huge mistake and Earth will come to regret it. Over.'

'It was out of my hands, Mark. General Gilby wants to speak to Doug. Over,' said Neil.

'Why Doug? Who is in charge of Moonbase? You told me I was the commander and Anna would be my deputy. Why are they wanting to speak to Doug? Over.' I said.

'You already know that, Mark, but hopefully it will be back to normal soon. How are Roy and the others recovering? Over,' said Neil.

'Fine,' I said. 'Here's Doug.'

'Hello, sir. Colonel Baker here. Over.'

'What is the current situation, Colonel? Over,' said the general.

'The people from the rille have been dealt with. We are in total control of Moonbase and the Asimov Rille. I've a squad bringing some equipment and furniture back from the rille as we speak. The habitat is worth maintaining for scientific work, or even as an emergency solar flare shelter, according to Pete Hazel. Over.'

‘Well done, Colonel. You can hand over operations to Commander Noble, so that the entire facility can return to standard operations. Over.’

‘Some of the Chinese astronauts are hopping over to Ben Lei habitat in one of the Dragonstars. I’ve provided projectors in case there are bugs there too. Over,’ said Doug.

‘We have no problem with that, Colonel.’

Neil said, ‘I’ll pass on that information to Ms Liu and Mr Melapov. Bob is with us here. Over.’

‘I’d like to know why this action was taken, General,’ I said. ‘We had great success communicating with the infected and it was perfectly clear to us that the symbiosis was mutually beneficial. We also tested it with some of our own people and there were no adverse reactions whatsoever. The idea to set up a study section in the bio dome was the best solution, Over.’

‘Get real, Commander,’ said the General. ‘We had no way of telling whether they’d revert to type in order to conquer the Earth. We had no choice. Better to get it over and done with. Over.’

‘As far as I’m concerned, General, it was genocide of another intelligent species. Not only that, but it was the first alien life we have ever discovered… and *you* decided to eliminate it. I believe that to be a foolish and reprehensible decision. History will judge you severely! Over.’

'Well, Mr Noble, you can think what you like. As far as we are concerned, we have saved the Earth from invasion and recovered a valuable scientific facility. Your attitude is noted. If I have anything to do with it, you will regret your words, and this will be the end of your NASA career.'

'How dare you!' I said. The niceties of waiting for "over" cast aside in my anger.

There was a short break in the transmission, then Neil spoke, 'He's left the room, Mark. Speaking to him like that was not a great career move. Over.'

'After being undermined, frankly, I don't give a damn, Neil,' I said. 'I'm resigning from NASA on my return to Earth.'

'Don't be hasty,' said Bob Michaels. 'The general has no influence over who we decide to work with or employ.'

'We'll see,' I said, knowing I needed to be among the first to return to Earth. 'For now, I am planning to send personnel who are not required here back to Earth. I'll be returning with them. Over.'

'I'm sorry you feel like that, Mark. Let's talk about it when you return. Over,' said Neil.

'I'm with Neil on this,' said Bob.

'Nothing to talk about. Could you consider what your plans are for resuming the work at Moonbase? Bill and Anna feel exactly as I do and will be returning with me. Over.'

‘I will, Mark. I’m truly sorry about the action of the military. Over.’

‘What’s the latest from Amherst and Cambridge? Over.’

‘I’m meeting a delegation from both this afternoon. Over,’ said Neil.

‘Then you’ll probably realise what you have lost! Out,’ I said angrily and cut the transmission.

‘Well done,’ said Bill.

‘How’d it come over?’ I asked.

‘Brilliant,’ said Anna. ‘They hadn’t a clue. You should go into theatre.’ She laughed.

‘Sounded real to me,’ said Bill.

‘Great job, Doug,’ I said.

‘I’m still really uneasy about it. I’ve become a traitor to true humans,’ he said.

‘You seriously still concerned, Doug?’ I asked.

‘I could have murdered you when I realised what you’d done, but the calming, reasonableness of my entity soon found my areas of worry and settled them,’ said Doug.

‘Yes, she has a wonderful effect on my thoughts too,’ said Anna.

‘And, anyway,’ said Doug, ‘he’s just told me that I’m his hero!’

We all laughed.

‘Hard to think that just a week ago we saw them as enemies. Now the Earth is our enemy. A total turnaround,’ said Bill.

‘An inferior breed,’ I said. ‘We’re the future, but rather than stealing humankind’s future, we’re actually giving them access to the rest of the universe. It’s win-win for us all. They will soon realise this was the only way.’

∞∞∞∞∞∞∞∞∞∞∞

Five days later, the common room was packed. Everyone was there. I’d even broken the rule about the com dome always being manned. I left the computer to play answerphone.

I stepped up onto the small stage, which was sometimes used for karaoke, entertainment, or amateur dramatics. It probably wasn’t really necessary with the full complement of Moonbase usually being fewer than twelve people. Today, however, I looked out over a sea of more than thirty faces.

‘Thank you all for being here,’ I said. ‘I’m not a great one for speeches, but today I can see a group of likeminded people. We are all different, of course, but we all hold within us an entity who keeps us focused on what really matters.

‘Mary tells us we will soon be travelling to the stars. It has so augmented her astrophysics abilities that she now knows exactly how to build a starship. I, for one, want to be on board when we set out to leave the solar system. There are so many fascinating exoplanets with far more potential than Mars. Some might be habitable without suits and domes. Many of the thousands already found have liquid water if TESS is to be believed.'

[TESS = Transiting Exoplanet Survey Satellite, launched 18th April, 2018.]

I continued, 'Tosh tells me the entities have cures for most human diseases and we can all expect to double our remaining life expectancy. I dare say that would not have been possible if it hadn't been for Tosh's improved intellect with which he continually bludgeons the rest of us.'

The assembly laughed, even Tosh.

'We are the most fortunate humans. We have discovered another intelligent race,' I said.

'Nah,' Tosh shouted out, 'they discovered us!' More laughter.

'Now we're to set off on a great adventure, to enhance all of our fellow humans. To give everyone the opportunity to learn more about, firstly themselves, then our world and finally the universe. Space travel will become simpler and more accessible and, with our new abilities and clarity of thought, war and conflict should quickly become a thing of the past.

'Most of us will be on Earth in a few days. We know we must be careful only to give away the secret of our new intellect to those we are enhancing. That will be someone new every two or three days. Those divided entities will know all that is known by their other halves and so will take over their hosts without pain and will quickly inform them of the wonderful lives they will be able to live.

'Take care, everyone, but go eagerly and fearlessly into the future.'

Applause rang out and we all mingled for the last time. More than half of us were to leave Moonbase in the morning.

29 Return To Earth

Six of us stood by Dragonstar 3. Me, Anna, Bill, Doug, Tosh and Mary. We'd filled the storage section with items which needed returning home and now took our last look around the surface of the moon.

Once sealed in, my enhanced memory took over and I anticipated all of the communications between Anna and the Gateway.

'Ignition, one, zero!' said the computer.

The Dragonstar lifted off far faster than one would normally expect. The moon's weak gravity was a major factor in the speed of the ascent. Thirty minutes later, the Gateway was alongside us and we were soon docked and floating in through the tunnel in the top of the Dragonstar vehicle to the Gateway. My entity briefly flashed a memory of the fun I'd had in this space with Linda. In my mind I told him to shut up and we began the preparation of an Orion to take us home.

Although Orions were more comfortable with four or five astronauts, we wanted to return together. It would be a squeeze for six, but we were prepared for a few days discomfort.

Anna spoke to NASA, agreed our separation time and a steady application of thrust saw us en route to the blue marble we could often see through the porthole. My entity kept directing my gaze towards it. He was even more excited than I.

The moon drifted away from us, or so it seemed, as the journey to Earth began. In three days, we'd be floating in the Pacific off San Diego and the navy would be lifting us out of the water. Far more nauseating than free fall.

As the capsule bobbed sickeningly, we all looked at each other and confirmed that Tosh's "vaccination" had worked its wonders. All our entities had survived with only minor ill effects.

We were not allowed to open our capsule and had to wait until the crane on the support ship could lift us out and onto the warship deck where it was immediately irradiated.

Once we emerged, we too were irradiated, as were the interior and storage areas of the capsule. No chances were being taken. My entity did not feel so bad this time. Tosh had told us resistance would improve.

When I was alone with Bill, I said, 'That was worrying.'

'Yes, they might have found some stronger radiation,' he said.

'Fortunately not,' I replied.

The captain invited us to dinner in his cabin with the first officer. By the time we left, two extremely senior navy officers were enjoying their entities' benefits. I retained my divided entity for an even more special connection ashore. Tosh had a flask containing at least another thirty entities with which he intended to enhance key individuals at NASA.

The following day, on the quay, I could see Linda. I couldn't wait to hold her in my arms. My entity was excited about her condition. He wanted to see whether he could interact with a child in the womb. He assured me he'd take care.

We hugged and were soon back in the hotel. Our first private kiss gave her more than just a loving feeling. I held her tight, steadying her as my entity's twin entered her and introduced herself.

She immediately checked Linda's health and that of the embryo and told us all was right with the world.

∞∞∞∞∞∞∞∞∞∞∞

Four weeks later, the number of augmented humans had grown into the hundreds of thousands. In three months, almost everyone on Earth would belong to the new breed of humankind.

The world would change and adapt. I was hoping our exploration of the universe would become a greater priority, and disease, poverty and conflict would become part of history.

Enhanced humankind was facing a new future and I wanted to be part of it.

Linda's bump was beginning to show and already had its own entity. Our little family was benefiting enormously from their having become part of us, and no, we didn't need to evict them to the dressing table when we made love. They enhanced everything!

I received a call from Neil, who I'd personally augmented during my "resignation meeting" the first week back. 'Mark. Is a month's vacation, a long enough break?'

'Why? What do you have in mind?' I asked.

'How would you like an interstellar space jaunt?'

'Mary's cracked the problems then?'

'She has,' he said.

'What's the mission?'

'Trappist-1. You up for it?' he asked.

The phone was on hands-free. I looked at Linda and she nodded.

'Count me in,' I said.

'Better come in tomorrow then. You'll want to assist with the design and pick your crew.'

END

∞∞∞∞∞∞∞∞∞∞∞∞∞∞∞∞∞∞∞∞

So ends the beginning. Learn more about the effect of the entities on the people of Earth when you join Mark Noble on the next expedition – the voyage to visit TRAPPIST-1, with its cluster of rocky planets including several in the Goldilocks Zone, and one which is thought to have liquid water.

[NASA/Caltech artist's impression of six of the Trappist-1 worlds.]

Sign up for the newsletter below to be advised when Trappist-1 is released.

A Word from Tony

Thank you for reading MOONSTRUCK. Reviews are very important for authors and I wonder if I could ask you to say a few words on the review page where you purchased this book. Every review, even if it is only a few words with a star rating, helps the book move up the rankings.

Tony's Books

Currently, I have written seven science fiction stories. Federation is the first of a trilogy and Moonstruck is the second in a series about astronaut Mark Noble. All my books can be found at https://harmsworth.net including signed paperbacks.

THE DOOR, already a UK Kindle bestseller in two categories: Henry Mackay and his dog regularly walk alongside an ancient convent wall. Today, as he passes the door, he glances at its peeling paint. Moments later he stops dead in his tracks. He returns to the spot, and all he sees is an ivy-covered wall. The door has vanished!

He unwittingly embarks on an exciting trail of events with twists, turns, quantum entanglement and temporal anomalies. It becomes an unbelievable adventure to save humanity which you'll be unable to put down.

The Door is an intriguing and unique science fiction mystery.

Discover the astonishing secrets being concealed by The Door today!

FEDERATION takes close encounters to a whole new level. A galactic empire of a quarter of a million worlds stumbles across the Earth. With elements of a political thriller, there is an intriguing storyline which addresses the environmental and social problems faced by the world today.

The aliens' philosophy on life is totally unexpected. With the help of intelligent automatons, they've turned what many on Earth felt was a reviled political system into a utopia for the masses, but are they a force for good or evil, and will the wealthy make the compromises needed for a successful outcome?

A Daragnen university graduate, Yol Rummy Blin Breganin, discovers that Earth failed in its attempt to join the Federation, and, for some unknown reason, members are forever banned from visiting or contacting the planet. Rummy had never heard of a whole world being outlawed. Perhaps it would be sensible to leave well enough alone but no, he decides to investigate…

Some readers have considered this series some sort of left-wing propaganda, but it isn't. It is a story, a work of imagination and should be read as such. However, if you have trouble telling science fiction from reality, or if your political convictions are so fanatical that you can never see the 'other point of view' then you might be better reading my other books.

FEDERATION is the first in the trilogy. The second volume, FEDERATION AND EARTH is also available. HIDDEN FEDERATION is due out in June 2020. The trilogy has been compared with the writing of Asimov and Banks.

Submerge yourself in humankind's cultural and economic dilemma with FEDERATION.

MINDSLIP: The radiation from Betelgeuse turning supernova causes every creature on Earth to swap minds! Men to women, children to adults, animals to humans, old to young, and vice versa. How would you handle changing sex or species? Mindslip combines frightening science fiction with psychological anguish.

The change in astrophysicist Geoff Arnold is challenging, and his wife and children have vanished. He joins the government's catastrophe committee with the brief to find a solution to Mindslip before it completely destroys society and the economy.

Millions die! Billions survive danger, harassment and abuse, and manage to adapt to their change of species, race, sex, and age. Geoff discovers that the change his wife has experienced is life-threatening. Can he juggle his new life, help save the world and rescue his wife in time?

This stand-alone work is unique. Science fiction with elements of soft horror, all in the style of the old masters. A real page-turner. I've been told that this is reminiscent of the late, great John Wyndham's masterpieces.

Become part of the bizarre, yet realistic world of MINDSLIP. Its reviews are the best of all of my books.

MOONSCAPE: We've known that the moon is dead since Apollo. But what if something lay dormant in the dust, waiting to be found?

In 2028, Mark Noble is conducting a survey of a moon crater. An entity secretly grabs a ride back to Moonbase on Mark's buggy. Once in the habitat, it begins to infect the crew. They find themselves in a frightening, helter-skelter adventure with only two possible outcomes: losing or saving the Earth.

MOONSCAPE is the first in a series of hard science fiction stories featuring Mark Noble. If you like fast-paced adventure, fraught with the additional dangers found in space, then this tale has been written especially for you.

Explore the page-turning world of MOONSCAPE today! MOONSTRUCK, the second in the Mark Noble series is also now available. The third book TRAPPIST-1 will be available during 2020.

THE VISITOR, already a UK Kindle bestseller in three categories and now an exciting audiobook: Specialist astronaut Evelyn Slater encounters a small, badly damaged, ancient, alien artefact on the first ever space-junk elimination mission. Where was it from? Who sent it?

International governments impose a security clampdown. Evelyn leads a team of hand-picked scientists who make amazing discoveries within the alien device. Secrecy becomes impossible to maintain. When the news is finally released, she becomes embroiled in international politics, worldwide xenophobic hatred, and violence.

This is book one of my loosely connected First Contact series of novels. If you like realistic near-future stories which compel you to imagine yourself as the protagonist, The Visitor is the book for you.

THE VISITOR – hard science fiction with a wicked twist. Buy it now and be transported into orbit.

Non-Fiction by Tony Harmsworth

LOCH NESS, NESSIE & ME: Almost everyone, at some point in their lives, has wondered if there was any truth in the stories of monsters in Loch Ness? Loch Ness, Nessie & Me answers all the questions you have ever wanted to ask about the loch and its legendary beast.

In these 400 pages with more than 200 pictures, including the famous ones, and illustrations, you will find a geography of Loch Ness, a travel guide to the area, a biography of its mythical inhabitant; and an autobiography of the man who set up the Loch Ness Centre, worked with many of the research groups, and helped coordinate Operation Deepscan. Me!

Explore the environmental and physical attributes of Loch Ness which make certain monster candidates impossible. Find detailed explanations of how pictures were faked and sonar charts, badly interpreted. Learn how Nessie has affected the people and businesses which exist in her wake, and suspend belief over the activities of the monstrous monks of Fort Augustus Abbey.

My involvement at the loch has lasted over forty years, including creating increasingly sceptical exhibitions, dioramas and multi-media shows. This is the first comprehensive book to be penned by someone who lives overlooking the loch. It is essential for anyone interested in Loch Ness and the process of analysing cryptozoological evidence.

Now's the time to discover the truth about this mystery, once and for all. Get your copy today!

SCOTLAND'S BLOODY HISTORY: Ever been confused about Scotland's history – all the relationships between kings and queens, both Scottish and English?

Why all the battles, massacres and disputes? Scotland's Bloody History simplifies it all.

Discover the history of Scotland from prehistoric man to the current Scottish Nationalist government. Follow the timeline from the Stone Age, through the Bronze Age and the Iron Age. Find out about the Picts, the Scots, the Vikings and the English. Learn about the election of Scotland's early kings and how Shakespeare maligned one of our finest monarchs.

In simple, chronological order, this book will show you how the animosity between England and Scotland grew into outright warfare including tales of Braveheart and wars of independence.

I have taken the bloodiest events of the last three thousand years and used them to clarify the sequence of events. Don't buy this book to learn the boring stuff, this book is packed with action from page one to the final three words which might haunt you over the next decade.

Robert the Bruce, Mary Queen of Scots, the Stewarts and Jacobites. It is all there. Explore Scotland's Bloody History now!

Tony Harmsworth's Reader Club

Building a relationship with my readers is the very best thing about being a novelist. In these days of the internet and email, the opportunities to interact with you is unprecedented. I send occasional newsletters which include special offers and information on how the series are developing. You can keep in touch by signing up for my no-spam mailing list.

Sign up at my webpage: https://harmsworth.net/ or on my https://facebook.com/lochnesstony and you will know when my books are released and will get free material from time to time and other information.

If you have questions, don't hesitate to write to me at Tony@Harmsworth.net.

Printed in Great Britain
by Amazon

46796621R00145